LOAD OF MERCY

A NOVEL

~ **FreshAroma** ~

Load Of Mercy

Chanetsa G Mazarura

A ~ **FreshAroma** ~ book
Published in the United Kingdom by Balancing Rocks
Publications Limited

www.balancingrockspublications.co.uk

'If the gods have given you a wound, it is so that flies may feast upon your flesh'

- Shona proverb

One

Run-away father

Tears pour down her cold cheeks like rivers. Cold sweat slides down her brow and collects into teary eyes. Head bowed and hands furiously clutching the brown and cream duvet, her legs quake and knock against each other at the knees. She watches him through the small cracks in the wooden door as he jumps onto his old bicycle and rides away, whistling like he always does when he is in a good mood, buckling his belt with both hands and balancing his butt onto the seat as if nothing at all has happened. Frozen pain climbing up her spine, her silent cry turns into weeping. She gathers into her hands the beautiful dress which Tete Tarisayi brought her from the city. It is now a mess.

'Why God, why?' she mutters to herself.

The humming which approaches from the direction of the village hills drawing close, she recognises the voice. Mother has come back early today. As leader of the church women's Ruwadzano Wing, RW, it is not unusual for her to spend the entire Saturday afternoon at the church. She is a respected and clever woman, decent, oftentimes used as the standard of perfection by the drunk men of the village when they bash their wives in the dead of the night. It is not uncommon, the bashing of one's own wife. The women accept it as part of the hard work of building a home, something which the men have to do now and again in order to assert their manliness. After all, no man can stand the embarrassment of an untrained wife. Mother is proud of her reputation, and Father brags about having clinched the most virtuous woman of their time, choosing to refer to himself as 'Mai Mercy's husband' instead of his own name.

On the other hand, and unlike Mother, Father attends church only during the now common funerals, he considers it advance payment for that time when he shall be called to be with his ancestors in the heavens. When that time comes, he wants the church to bury him and a big cross like the one on his late father's grave, Sekuru Chigodho's, planted on his own. Following which he wants all the rituals which will cause him to be accepted by the ancestors, including the *bira*, done for him, otherwise he would come back to haunt those left behind.

'Mercy,' Mother calls as soon as she is in the yard and as she walks to the kitchen hut to put down the reed basket balanced on her pleated head. She pushes ajar the slightly open kitchen door using her behind and enters inside, ducking so as to avoid hitting against the wooden frame. She is in there for a moment, and when she comes out, her bible and hymn-book still in her hands, she walks towards Mercy's hut and continues humming to herself. 'Mercy!' she calls again, but there is no reply. 'Where is this girl?' she asks, then continues singing. *Ndinoshamiswa kwazvo*; that is the name of the hymn.

Mercy doesn't respond. She battles to suppress the weeping, pressing her lips together whilst boiling on the inside. She sits there, in their bedroom, her brain numb and heavy. Confused.

Mother flings open the metal door to Mercy's hut and picks up her daughter's black purse from the floor. 'She could not possibly have left this,' she says to herself, then she starts calling after Mercy in a louder voice as she pops out of the hut, like she always does when Mercy is at Chipo's home, which is a little less than a mile away. She walks towards the bedroom hut that she shares with Father, gingerly, her voluptuousness dancing and clapping with each step in a somewhat rhythmical fashion, a phenomenon which increases her desirability to the men of the village who oftentimes are mesmerised by her movement that they turn their heads several times when they pass her on the footpath, inviting furious ridicule from their offended wives.

'This man, he just left the door like this, not properly closed,' Mother complains. 'Men! Sometimes you have to treat them like kids,' she says as she shakes her head sideways and pushes the door inwards. 'Mercy!' she exclaims when, as she opens the door, she comes face to face with her daughter crying with her face buried in her hands, in the same position she has been since Father left the compound a while ago.

'What happened?' Mother asks, picking up a small piece of cloth lying on the floor with the tips of her fingers, scanning the walls of the dark room as if looking for a clue. A lizard sprints across the wall and rests by the edge of the thatched roof, its light green throat heaving up and down, looking down at them without any fear. Safe.

Mother walks to Mercy and sits by her side on the squeaky wooden bed. 'What is it? What are you doing in your father's bedroom?' she asks, tossing the cloth back to the floor as if shaking off a chameleon from her finger.

Mercy doesn't answer. Neither does she stop crying. The tears spatter onto the dusty floor, which is finished with clay that has now developed notable cracks.

It takes a while before it hits Mother what could have happened. She hugs her daughter, tightly: 'Don't tell me he did this to you Mercy... did he? Did he, Mercy? Tell me my daughter ... did your father do this to you?'

Mercy nods her head and bursts into fresh tears, shaking and trembling and burying her head deep into Mother's lap as if she is to sink right into her. Mother clasps her hands against the back of her own head and wails, muttering unintelligible words like the crazy man of the village, Jekiseni. 'How could he? Oh God, how could he?' she keeps asking the wind.

Mother is deeply hurt. She kneels on the side of the bed as if to pray, then gets up to her feet and reaches into the old wardrobe as if looking for something, rummages through her and Father's clothes, and pulls down the wire hangers and scatters them all over the floor. She slumps back onto the bed and hugs her daughter, closing her eyes and pressing against her thumping chest, feeling the warmth of her half-naked body. She is hurt because Mercy is their only child. Hurt because they had waited for a long time when she came, so much that Father could not easily accept that she was his own child when it happened. He thought then, that Mother could have got herself impregnated by another man, a relative perhaps, in order to please him. It took a great deal of convincing from Sekuru Chigodho and the comments which people made regarding Mercy's resemblance to him, for him to accept her as his own. Then he adored her and, together with Mother, emptied all his love onto the one child. She is now a beautiful girl, a serial heartbreaker famed for turning down lots of boys. She has never doubted her parents' love, until a few moments ago, when she was just getting ready to go to the village centre with Chipo, when Father called her into his bedroom and she came running.

'Where did he go?' Mother asks as she tries to be calm. She wipes off tears from her eyes using the edge of her red and blue church uniform.

'I don't know. He left on his bicycle,' Mercy says as she also wipes off the tears and continues looking down, forcing her arms into the sleeves of the torn dress, covering her tiny breasts.

She is ashamed.

'What exactly happened?' Mother asks again, looking into Mercy's eyes.

Mercy fights back the tears as she narrates her ordeal, then she cracks, crying helplessly and struggling to get the words out of her mouth. She uses the yellow dress to wipe away the tears.

When she is done, Mother says, calmly, 'Why did you agree to come into your father's bedroom, Mercy? You know you shouldn't've done that.'

'But he called me, *mama*. What was I supposed to do? Ignore him?' she asks, lifting up her teary eyes to look at her.

'I've told you over and again that men are animals. Now, look at what has happened. What is that you are wearing anyway?'

'Just my dress, *mama*,' she replies, holding the edge of the dress and confused as to why Mother seems to want to blame her for this.

'You see now, Mercy, you see?' Mother says. Then she sighs.

'But he is my father, *mama*. How would I have known that he was going to do that to me, his own daughter?'

Mercy is angry.

Mother opens up her mouth to speak but no words come out of her, she doesn't know what to say. They sit like that for some time, quietly.

There are footsteps outside, in the yard.

'Hello!' a woman's voice says. 'Mai Mercy, are you there?'

It is Mapudege, Mother's distant friend, not really a friend but one who only shows up in their home when she wants to borrow something, from food to shoes to earrings to pots, and at one point to be accompanied to her house by Father in the middle of the night because she was afraid. She is a loud mouth who sometimes attends Mother's church when she is in the mood. The RW women very much abhor her, they say that she prostitutes herself with every preacher that is assigned to the church, enticing them with her rather short and revealing dresses which she loves to wear and carelessly sit at the most front bench in the church, baring her goodies to the 'Men of God'. Mother does not believe these malicious lies against the Men of God. Not that she doesn't think that Mapudege is capable of such, but because the Men of God cannot possibly fall for that, at least not with this dirty creature that is so loose and loud that she is the first suspect in any case of infidelity in the lazy rural village.

'Mai Mercy,' Mapudege calls again, in a loud voice.

Mercy is about to answer, but Mother cups her hand against her mouth.

'Mai Mercy, are you there?' Mapudege continues. She walks to the kitchen hut and sits by the open door, facing the one-roomed square hut that serves as Mother and Father's bedroom, where Mercy and Mother are and can clearly see her through the half open door. Mapudege cannot see them because of the lack of light streaming into the room. 'I will wait here for you, if you think that I will go away without getting what I came here for. Or I will just help myself and you will have to follow me to my house,' she says, but more to herself.

'You can't let people know about this,' Mother whispers to Mercy. 'What would they say?'

'But, *mama...*' Mercy tries to protest.

'Shhhhhhh. No. He is your father. You can't let this news get into that blabbermouth's hands. This is an internal matter. No-one should know about this, Mercy, not the RW women. We will fix this on our own, as a family.'

Mercy is confused. She keeps wanting to say something, but Mother's hand is firm against her mouth. She gives up and lets out a constipated sigh as the tears roll down again.

Mother peeps through the door in time to see Mapudege push open the door to the kitchen hut. She disappears inside for a moment, then comes out with the basket which Mother brought with her just moments ago, looks around as if to make sure that nobody is looking, closes the door carefully and begins to walk away from the compound at a fast pace.

Mother is furious. She leaves Mercy alone on the bed and dashes out of the house to run after her. 'Mapudege!' she calls after her, but Mapudege continues walking, unperturbed. 'Mapudege, I know you can hear me,' Mother says as she literally runs after her.

Mapudege stops in her tracks, puts the basket down without looking back and takes to her heels, Mother shouting after her: 'God will punish you Mapudege, you and whoever dips his thingy into yours. You think you can just walk into my compound and grab whatever you like, eh? If I leave you like this, next time you will come after my husband's thingy. What kind of a woman are you?'

Mapudege makes a turn and disappears behind the bushes without turning her head even once. Mother shakes her head, claps her hands in exasperation, and laughs sarcastically. She picks up the basket with the few items she bought from the kiosk at the school where the RW holds its meetings and heads back to the homestead, tears silently watering her face.

In the evening, when she passes by Mercy's house on her way from the village centre, Chipo is still at a loss as to why Mercy has suddenly fallen sick when she was perfectly fine in the morning, when they took a bath together in Mupfurati River and planned to go to the village centre. It was not easy leaving her behind. Mercy's boyfriend, Freedom, was not happy, which is quite unusual and does not suit him at all. He seemed worried to the bone and must have felt awkward walking around the few shops and the market in the company of Chipo and Lovemore, like he was causing a sort of disharmony or imbalance. He called it quits, finally, and went back to his home in the neighbouring village since he couldn't visit Mercy because of Father, who is well known for his strictness and who, in fact, has no single clue that his daughter now has a boyfriend.

'I have to go now, Mai Mercy, before it gets too dark,' Chipo says to Mother. She picks up her little self from the mat and her purse from the floor before gently patting Mercy on the shoulder. 'I hope you get better my friend,' she says.

For a moment, Mercy remains quietly seated on the mat by the fire, as if in deep thought. Father is on a stool just across from her, on the other side of the fire, occasionally spreading his hands to the heat and rubbing them together. Mother opens the lid of the big black pot which is on the fire, on the hearth in the middle of the hut, puts it back on and blows into the fire with her mouth to fan it. It is a bit chilly tonight, and the silence in the room is deafening.

Chipo is about to step out of the hut when Mercy says, 'I will see you out…'

'No, Mercy,' Mother quickly interjects, passing a quick glance at Father before locking her eyes with Mercy's in a telling manner. 'You need to rest. I am sure Chipo will be fine. Besides, she has to rush home to cook for her father. I know you two when you meet, it's hard to separate you.'

Mercy simply ignores Mother's plea. She drags herself up and staggers to the door, and out, feeling a little dizzy. For a moment, she can't see where she is going. Her head is spinning around.

'Are you alright?' Chipo asks as she holds her by the hand. 'Yes.'

Mother stands by the entrance of the round hut, on the elevated platform, watching the two slowly drift away from the compound. Mercy is dragging her feet a little but she doesn't want Chipo to notice, so she tries hard to hide it.

'Don't go too far you two,' Mother calls after them.

Mercy doesn't look back but keeps walking, mild pain running down her legs. She ignores it. She doesn't know if she wants anyone to ever know what happened to her, but Chipo can tell that all is not well.

'Mercy, tell me the truth,' Chipo finally says when Mother melts back into the hut. 'Is it Freedom? Are you pregnant?'

'No, are you crazy?' Mercy responds, her voice not confident.

Chipo is convinced that something is up somewhere, that it has nothing to do with the so-called sickness. 'Then what is it?' she asks. 'You were all fine just this morning, excited, then all of a sudden you are not well. What really is happening, why did you not go to the clinic?'

'Don't worry about me. I am okay now.'

'You sure don't look okay to me. Tell me the truth my friend, something is bothering you. Is it your mother? Did she find out about Freedom? Did she say you couldn't go out? Is that it? Tell me please, please.'

They stop just a few meters from the homestead. Chipo looks right into Mercy's eyes and says, 'It's your father, isn't it? I know your mother would understand…'

Mercy bursts into fresh tears, letting go of all that she bottled up since Mother told her to keep her mouth shut.

Chipo stands there with her mouth gaping, not knowing what to say. 'Stop crying,' she finally says. 'It won't solve anything. I know you love Freedom. He is a good guy and he loves you very much. I am sure your parents will understand with time.'

Chipo thinks that she has cracked the equation, yet she is far from it. It's got nothing at all to do with Freedom, it has everything to do with Father and Mother and Mercy. But how does Mercy explain it? How does she tell her friend that her own father did that to her? Where does she even begin?

'I won't go out with Freedom anymore,' she says, finally.

'Is that all?'

'He raped me, Chipo,' the words escape out of her mouth very fast.

Chipo looks at her in horror, from the head all the way down to her toes as if she is looking for the evidence. She opens her mouth to speak, brings her hand up to her mouth, then asks, 'When, Mercy? When?'

'Not him.'

'Who then? Tell me who did this to you Mercy, so I can pluck out their manhood with my bare hands? Who was it?'

'Father did,' Mercy says, wiping her eyes using the back of her hand.

Chipo is bewildered. Her mind tries hard to process and to reconcile the information coming to it, to sort and to arrange this into something palatable. 'You mean to tell me that your father raped you, Mercy, that he took away your honour?'

'I don't know what to do.'

'Oh no, it's true. Does your mother know?'

Mercy nods her head.

'What did she say?'

'Nothing. What can she say Chipo, and what would it change? He is her husband, my father. She can't afford to have him go to jail. She can't carry the shame.'

'And you think you can?' Chipo asks, angrily. 'You mean to tell me that your mother is happy for you to carry this load all your life because she doesn't want her husband to go to jail? Because she wants to maintain a status? That's not right Mercy. Not right at all!'

Chipo is visibly angry. 'You have to let the elders know about this, and the police too,' she continues.

'I can't Chipo, I can't …'

'Yes, you can and you will. You will have to do this or else I will do it. If he could do this to you then how can he still be your father? What kind of a father does that to his own daughter? No, no, it can't go just like that. You have to get justice.'

'I can't, Chipo,' Mercy insists. 'I shouldn't've told you about this. What about me? Can you imagine the shame? What about Freedom?'

'What if he comes onto you again, what will stop him from doing it again? It's not only taboo, but it's unfair, immoral. Cruel. Surely, this can't happen in this village. Chief Kamutsi must know about this.'

'Let's talk tomorrow, I beg you,' says Mercy. 'I am too confused. I don't know whether I am going or coming, whether I am alive or dreaming or dead. I need to think straight.'

'Alright then, sleep over it my friend. I will always be here for you,' Chipo says. She hugs Mercy as tears trickle down her cheeks too.

When Mother slides back into the hut, she confronts Father, 'What have you done, Petros? You have killed your daughter my husband, your own daughter…'

'How could you say that, Mai Mercy?' Father asks, looking into Mother's round eyes with his red and bulging ones. 'Do you think that I enjoyed it? You know it had to be done…'

'You shouldn't've done it … you shouldn't. How will you ever live with your daughter in the same house again? How will you look into her eyes? You have killed her literally, literally killed her.'

'Shut up, woman! Don't say that I have killed my daughter as if you were not in on it, don't put this all on me,' Father says in a voice full of anger. He pounds his fist against the metal hearth and stamps his feet against the ground, overturning Mother's pot into the raging fire.

'What if she speaks, if she tells her friends? You know that Chipo girl is too clever. What if the Reverend gets to know about this? Oh, I am finished, totally finished. If that blabbermouth, Mapudege, gets wind of this then finish, the end, end of story. How do I face the RW?'

'Then you better talk to your daughter, woman. Knock some sense into her…'

He does not finish his statement as Mercy walks back into the compound. When she enters the hut, she sits on the mat next to Mother, facing Father.

Father clears his throat and begins to say, 'Mercy, my daughter…'

She doesn't allow him to finish his statement. She draws out a burning log from the fire and hurls it at him, spinning, catching him on the chin and chest and falling him off his stool, backwards. 'You are not my father, you bastard!' she cries as she attempts to launch at him again with another. She feels like killing him, like pouring the hot water on the fire onto his face and poking his eyes with a metal fork.

Mother pulls her back down and holds her tightly against her chest, Father getting up and starting for the door. He looks back at her and wipes off a tear from his left eye.

'Stop pretending!' Mercy is furious. 'Stop it!'

'You know that I ... I can explain ... I...'

'I hate you! I hate you!'

Father walks out of the hut, leaving Mercy in a fit of rage and Mother trying to calm her down. He takes his bicycle and rides into the dark without saying where he is going.

'Where are you going?' Mother calls after him but he doesn't respond. He disappears into the darkness as Mercy and Mother hug one more time.

Two

Prodigal son

Three weeks have passed since he left. Mother is worried although she won't admit to it. She carries on as if everything is hunky-dory, cleaning up and dressing up, and eating herself up on the inside, smiling to all and sundry. To cover up, she forges a story, one that she knows Mapudege would run with without a single shred of evidence. 'Father travelled to Harare because his cousin had a baby boy,' she tells Mapudege.

Mapudege doesn't disappoint. She goes on a whirlwind with the good news, adding that it was her that accompanied Father to the bus terminus because she is Mother's best friend, that the baby will be named Chigodho after his late grandfather. A few days later, and shamelessly, she makes an about turn after some people come back to the village claiming to have seen Father wandering aimlessly in what used to be the white commercial farming district some hundred kilometres away. She is quick to attest to the truthfulness of the new story, stating that Father never stopped cycling and is now like a mad man. Mother refutes these assertions with all her might, blaming Mapudege and the evil people of the village for concocting stupid tales.

Mother's denial doesn't last long, however, as Father finally shows up in the fourth week without his famed bicycle, stinky and in rags, like the returning prodigal son preached about at Mother's church a few days ago. Although he does not come in the cover of darkness as she had hoped, Mother is lucky to be not at home when it happens. But many of the villagers witness it, with great amazement and amusement, lining up along the hedges of their sandy fields in the early hours of the Saturday morning to catch a glimpse of the run-away father.

Mercy is sitting lazily at the entrance of the kitchen hut when she sees him from a distance. She recognises him immediately because of the slight limp in his walk. His frame is so wasted that she has difficulty accepting that it is him. She gets up to her feet, hastily, to make sure. There is a clamping inside her tummy. She looks at him again and feels pity, but rage takes over when she relives the circumstances of his leaving, inviting back the pain and hatred that she is desperately trying to get over. She runs into her hut and locks the door from the inside.

When Mother comes back the news has already reached her ears. She doesn't stop to talk to anyone on the way. No-one talks to her either. They just stare at her and at each other with talking eyes. At home, she finds that Father has now had a bath and changed his clothes, and is sitting on a stool just outside their bedroom hut, casting a lonely figure and suddenly looking much older. She can't believe that three weeks away from her food can make a man this skinny, like one that has not eaten anything in a year. She doesn't talk to him or greet him, but simply puts down the water bucket she is carrying on her head close to the wooden plates-rack in the middle of the yard, disappears into the kitchen and comes back with half a green bar of soap and a dish full of dirty plates. She scrubs these vigorously until they are spick-and-span, without saying a word, spreads them onto the rack and goes back into the kitchen to cook a late breakfast. She bakes the traditional hard flour-and-mealie-meal cake using a makeshift oven fired by wood. When it is ready, she takes some to Mercy's hut and some to her husband, with Tanganda tea. Father quietly gobbles down the food without lifting up his head. He is ashamed.

It is well after midday when Mercy finally emerges from her hut without having eaten any of the food and sits just outside the door. Father is washing his clothes in a green plastic bucket just outside his bedroom and Mother is sweeping the already clean kitchen floor with a soft broom made of dry grass. It is the first-time Mercy is witnessing Father do a household chore, other than when she has seen him polishing his old boots to go after the popular *seven-days* brew in neighbouring villages. She walks up to him and says, 'Hello, *baba*.'

He looks up at her, slowly, and says in a rather dry and weak voice, 'I am sorry my daughter.' He looks down again and continues washing his clothes, scrubbing these against both hands.

Mercy does not say anything else. She walks up to the kitchen hut and sits by the door. Mother brings a plate full of raw groundnuts and sits next to her. They silently crack open the shells and pop the contents into their mouths, one after the other.

'Where have you been, Petros?' Mother asks, finally.

Father does not reply. He rinses his clothes and takes them to the wireline behind the huts where he spreads them out without any hangers. When he comes back from there, he walks up to Mercy and kneels on both knees next to her, like a woman. 'Forgive me my child,' he says.

'Why did you do it, *baba*, why?'

'It was a terrible mistake my daughter, a work of the devil … I don't know what came over me … I will do everything, anything I can to make things right.'

'You think you can make it right, huh, that you can wipe out a piece of the past just like that and pretend that it never happened, huh? Will you hand me back my virginity? Will you?' she charges.

'Please let it go my daughter,' Mother says. 'After all is said and done, he is still your father. What he did is not right, but he is your father still, holding this against him will not help you in any way. Can't you see the shame on his face? Please my daughter, have a heart … a forgiving heart.'

Mercy is quiet for a while as she ponders. It is true, the shame on Father's face, like a man who has grown breasts on his forehead, like one who has been caught defecating in the chief's field in broad daylight. She had vowed to get him arrested when he came back, whenever that was going to be, and Chipo encouraged her, urging her to do the right thing. But seeing Father like this changes everything, it breaks and somewhat thaws her heart. She is not sure anymore what right means, whether getting Father thrown in jail is the right thing to do, whether she will be able to live with it.

Father continues kneeling in the sand like an ugly man begging a beautiful woman for marriage. When he opens his mouth again he says, 'Look, my daughter, I am ready to face my sin. You see, when I was away, I thought of taking my own life, but then I thought of you. I couldn't leave like this, you see, without having said my apologies. I want you to know that I love you, you see, that I have always loved you like a daughter, my only child. What I did is already done, I cannot undo it, so I can go to jail if that is what you want. I will hand myself over … but please forgive me my child. That is all that I ask for.'

With this, he begins to get up to his feet.

The words hit Mercy hard and somehow, despite her vow to not be fooled by whatever Father might say, she believes him. She reaches out her hand and touches his shoulder. 'No, *baba*, you won't go to jail,' she says, 'but you can't do that again, ever.'

Mother smiles. 'You are doing the right thing my daughter, the right thing...,' she says.

Tears in her eyes, Mercy gets up and locks herself up in her hut for the rest of the afternoon and night.

Mercy and Chipo are coming from church. Mercy is still trying to come to terms with Father's return and her decision to let him go. Faith and hope say that she has done the right thing, but her mind says otherwise. She has to be strong, she tells herself, like the Lord Jesus Christ who endured a lot of suffering when they spat at him and nailed him to the cross even after he had healed them and excited them with his miracles. Life is not fair, she thinks. It has never been.

'Your father came back?' Chipo asks.

'Yes,' replies Mercy. She knows very well what is coming next, and she is not ready for it. She doesn't have an answer.

'So?'

'So what?'

'You know what I mean, Mercy. He has to be punished for what he did to you.'

'I will not do that Chipo,' Mercy says with a straight face that shocks Chipo out of her wits.

'You are joking, right? Is your mother doing this to you?' Chipo doesn't understand.

'It's my decision, Chipo. He is my father and I am the victim,' Mercy explains, her mind converging with the words out of her mouth, waking up to the fact that indeed she is the victim, that no one else has a right to tell her what to do.

'Listen to yourself … I can't let you do this to yourself … Why?'

Chipo is upset.

They continue their quarrel as they walk towards Chipo's homestead. Chipo's father, Mangwiro, is in the fields looking after the cattle, and her brother, Francis, is not at home. Their mother died when they were still little, days after she received a thorough beating from Mangwiro which resulted in her taking her own life. Chipo, who is the older of the two, at that time was only three. She vaguely remembers having had a mother, although she is familiar with her face from the one picture which Mangwiro keeps in the blue folder in his bedroom, which Chipo has found him holding and crying over many times, alone. She and Francis have no clue what caused their mother's death, all they know is that Mangwiro has always been there for them. They have the utmost respect for their father.

'Good afternoon, Mr Mangwiro,' Mercy says in greeting.

'Good afternoon my child. How are you?' Mangwiro replies as he hurls a stone to drive away one of the cows that is about to cross the hedge. He whistles and it turns back into the fold. 'How is your father?' he continues.

'He is alright. He came back yesterday.'

'That's good. Tell him that I will come see him tonight.'

'Good afternoon, *baba*,' Chipo says.

'Yes, my daughter,' replies Mangwiro. 'Your food is on the shelf in the kitchen.'

'Thank you, *baba*,' Chipo says with a smile, but her mind is faraway. She really thinks that Mercy is making a mistake.

Mercy wishes Father was like Mangwiro, that he also helped with the household chores, sometimes. It is unheard of, however, that a whole man with a beard sits on the fire to cook a meal, using the same pots used by the women. It is for weak men, like Mangwiro. Impotent men. Men who have no idea how to exert their authority and earn the respect of their wives and children. Real men ensure that everyone works hard in the fields so there is no lack in the house, and that the food is always cooked well enough. And, when not in the fields, they chase after the traditional *seven-days* beer, allowing enough space for the women to cook and bath the children, to clean the house and to be ready for sex when they come back home in the middle of the night. Drunk.

Mangwiro is not like that. Well, he is no longer like that. The death of his wife dealt him a good blow. It turned around his life. The men of the village make fun of him, for behaving like a woman, a man stuck in household chores despite having grown-up children. If his wife was still alive, they would have said that he overdosed from her love portions. He doesn't care. Besides, having had a stint as a mechanic in Marondera, he is the only one in the village with another life skill apart from the peasant farming. Occasionally, when a truck or even the public bus, breaks down, they come looking for him. It is here, in his 'workshop' just outside the yard and close to the cattle pens, which is made of discarded rusty metal, that he spends his time dismantling and reassembling different equipment from discarded vehicles when Francis is looking after the cattle.

When she gets home, Mercy finds Tete Tarisayi sitting with Father in the shade of the mango tree in the middle of the yard. Father is on his wooden stool whilst Tete is on a reed mat. Tete, who is Father's only sister and remaining sibling after their two brothers died during the war of liberation many years ago, is not married and has no children. She lives in the city of Mutare, which is located by the country's eastern border with Mozambique.

'Aunty, is that you?' Mercy says, a wide smile painted across her face as she embraces with Tete. 'You just go and go for good aunty, are you sure? How could you do that?'

Tete smiles and gets up on her knees to hug her. 'Look how big you have become, Mercy?' she says as she sits back down. 'You are looking more and more like your mother.'

'Is that so, aunty?'

'Of course, I can see that my brother is keeping you well fed,' she continues. 'Where is your mother?'

'Ah aunty, you know *mama*, she is busy with all this her RW business.'

'Of course,' Tete agrees, 'that is why she is the virtuous woman that she is. My brother was lucky to have got such a woman.'

Mercy sits next to Tete. She is so happy that she forgets, almost, about her many troubles.

'If it were not for school I would have said you come with me to the city,' Tete says.

'Yes, aunty…' Mercy agrees.

Father nods his head.

'Oh darling, I will come back for you on your school break,' Tete says. They hug one more time, then she smiles and says to Father, 'My brother, you look worried. See how you have lost so much weight? What is it that is eating you up?'

Father gets up to his feet and lights a cigarette. 'Nothing,' he says. 'I am okay.'

He begins walking away, towards the fields, slowly as if it hurts. He knows that it is only a matter of time before Tete gets wind of his having been away from home, and he doesn't want to imagine the grilling that he will get from her, which will infuriate him. He is a few meters into the fields when two of Chief Kamutsi's messengers race into the yard on their huge black bicycles. He stops to look at them and begins walking back to find out what they want. He shudders when he thinks about it, he reckons that they could be here for him. But how? For a moment, he considers taking to his heels, but he knows that would be stupid, he is way past his age and stands no chance at all with the two young men. In any case, he doesn't have the strength to even try.

The young men do not say a word to the women, they just disembark from their cycles and hastily walk towards Father, whose heart is pounding fast and furious. Urine escapes and freely runs down his leg, wetting his thin trousers. Tete and Mercy watch as the well-built young men brush past them. They are still in puzzlement when they grab Father by the arms and cuff his hands from behind.

'What is this my friends?' Father asks. 'What have I done?'

'You defiled your daughter,' the ugly one says.

Tete is shocked. She cannot believe her ears.

Mercy is in tears.

The men nudge Father forwards. He looks weak and tired.

When Mercy raises her head, she sees Chipo walk into the yard as Father is being dragged away, in-between the two young men who are back on their bikes.

'This is the right thing, Mercy,' Chipo says.

'Is it true, Mercy?' Tete asks, still in a state of shock. She feels her legs melt at the joints and she crumbles down to the sand and starts crying. 'Oh, my brother, my brother. How can this be my brother, my brother ...?

Three

It pours

Chief Kamutsi emerges through the arch, like a spirit, and all people rise up to their feet and bow their heads in honour. The guards flanking the door do the same, crossing their legs and taking off their feathered hats in unison. His humped figure edges towards the throne, his frail body balancing against his smooth mahogany staff. On his head is a green oval hat which barely covers his white hair, and in the furrow below his eyebrows darkle tiny brown eyes that can no longer see any further than a stone's throw away, the black of eye now cloudy like one who is blind. In spite of this, his people still love him, not only because he has been there for a long time but because he is fair and witty, an icon who has managed to keep the warring tribes together. Several of the village elders walk alongside him as he gently does it, his two sons sticking by his side to make sure he does not fall like what happened to the neighbouring Chief Chatunga, who not many days ago missed a step and crumbled down to the dust and had to be picked up by his youthful wife. They guide him to the throne, which is made of polished carved wood overlaid with fluffy cushions and cloths for comfort, which has pinned above it, against the baobab tree which is part of the enclosure, different animal skins and long cow horns which are smooth like polished ivory. He takes his seat first, then his two sons sit on either side of him, then the elders and the rest of the people.

Father sits on his crossed legs on the sand, close to the front, his head bowed and one of the guards, the tall one, standing by his side.

Chief Kamutsi takes time to make himself comfortable, and after what seems like eternity, when he beckons, the guard gives a nudge to Father, whose hands are still cuffed as if he might run away. Father struggles to his feet, biting the dust one time before the guard helps him up with one hand. He still doesn't lift up his head, he keeps looking down at the sand as if counting the tiny brown ants which are running around after their perfect trail has been unravelled.

A few rituals; clapping, a bit of snuff, chanting, and the proceedings begin.

The enclosure which is the court, whose walls are made of grass and reeds and whose shade is made of thatch which is partly held up by surrounding tree branches and partly by a few poles, is so full that some of the people are standing outside. Many of the villagers from the seven villages under Chief Kamutsi have come to witness the proceedings, to get it first-hand instead of waiting to be fed spiced up stories out of Mapudege's busy lips.

'Your Highness, the Great Chief Kamutsi, honourable princes, elders and headmen, and you all great people of Tateguru,' the most senior elder, Melusi, says when all have settled and after he bows his head to Chief Kamutsi. 'Standing before you is a man accused of the most despicable thing in our villages, a taboo punished by death during the time of our ancestors. This man, Petros, is well known to us and is respected by many, but for him to sleep with his own daughter and to deflower her is not something that we can ignore. It deserves the greatest punishment possible. Your Highness, this is the reason why this gathering has been convened in your precious presence, to seek your wise counsel and judgement and to obtain justice for the girl, who is also here, and for the girls of these our villages and beyond. Thank you.'

Melusi bows his head one more time, then takes his seat.

Chief Kamutsi is not moved by the praises. They don't excite him anymore. He knows very well that behind the praises is a hidden agenda, careful manoeuvring by the senior elders to position themselves, to try and deny his elder son the right to succeed him after he dies. He will not fall for it, so he plays along like a fool but privately instructs his sons on the politics of the tribes. He lifts his staff, slowly as if in pain, and points it at Father. He clears his throat and says, 'Petros, is this true? Do you have anything to say?'

Father does not lift up his head or say anything. His eyes remain fixed to the floor, busy tracing the embroidery of the mat Chief Kamutsi's feet are resting on.

Chief Kamutsi pauses for a moment, then says, slowly and with emphasis, 'Petros, do you not have a mouth? Did you or did you not do what they say? You know that silence in this court is not only disrespectful, it is an admission of guilt. It is in your best interests to tell us your side of the story or else you will be condemned.'

Still, Father does not say a thing.

The silence is sustained, until Tete slowly gets up to her feet clapping her cupped hands in the manner of women, then says, 'My chief and elders, please hear me...'

'Go ahead my daughter,' Chief Kamutsi says, relieved that someone has broken the silence. 'He is your brother after all,' he says.

'I came to the village only yesterday,' Tete begins, 'and I had barely sat down with my brother when the messengers came and arrested him right in front of my eyes. What they accuse him of is something that baffles me. I have spoken to my niece here, Mercy, and to my daughter-in-law, Mai Mercy, but none of them seems to say anything that makes sense, anything which implicates my brother. They do more crying than talking, and when I ask them they keep shaking their heads like elephants. My chief and elders, what evidence is there that my brother did this terrible thing? I know my brother, I grew up with him, so I need some evidence for me to truly believe that he is capable of such a crime. May this honourable court get to the bottom of this, for everyone's peace. Thank you.'

With these words Tete sits down, clapping her hands one more time.

'My daughter,' Chief Kamutsi says, 'you have spoken well. I hear you, and it is my duty to make sure that we are all satisfied, that justice is discharged. But, tell me my daughter, why should we attempt to measure a dead snake with rope when the snake itself is here? Your brother is here, your in-law is here, and your niece is also here. Melusi, please present to the court the evidence that you have.'

Quickly, Melusi jumps up to his feet. He requests that Chipo, who all along has been outside, be brought in to testify. She walks in with all eyes on her, and confidently makes her way to the middle of the court, facing Chief Kamutsi and the elders. Father lifts up his head for the first time to meet her eyes, his eyes as if they say 'please don't do this,' then he looks down again.

'Your Highness,' Melusi says, 'this, our daughter standing before you, is Chipo, the daughter of Mangwiro, our dear brother of the Ndorochena totem, a second cousin to Petros. She came to my house yesterday in the afternoon and told me all about Petros's crime, and I found it in the interest of justice to immediately alert you of this great travesty against our *hunhuism*. You know that this thing Petros is said to have done is not acceptable in this community, it is a taboo that would certainly anger the gods and shut the heavens. We do not want calamity to visit these lands. Everyone here knows that Petros was away for a whole month and that he was seen in lands very far from here. Now we know what he was running away from, why he came back looking like a stick. As you know, one cannot eat poison and be not poisoned by it. One cannot robe another's honey trap without inviting a good biting from the bees. I thank you my chief.'

Melusi takes his seat.

'Thank you,' Chief Kamutsi says. He looks at Chipo and says, 'Now my daughter, we need to know the truth, nothing but the truth. Please tell us what you know, what it is that led you here.'

With no fear or mincing of words, Chipo explains everything in accordance with what Mercy told her. She tells of how Mercy was reluctant to report the matter and why she took it upon herself to do so, to help her friend who is afraid of her father.

'Thank you my daughter, you may sit down now. I want to hear from the mother of the child. I want to know what Mai Mercy has to say about this. After all, she is a respected churchwoman.'

Mother stands up to her feet and thanks Chief Kamutsi and the elders. She wipes tears off her eyes with a handkerchief, then says, 'My chief and elders, please forgive me, but I do not have much to say. Yes, I was concerned when my husband did not immediately come back from his trip to Harare where he had gone to do his business, and many hurtful things were said by the people of this village; that my husband was now mad, that I bewitched him, and a lot other things I cannot even bring myself to say with my mouth. Now, everyone here knows me and my husband. I am a churchwoman, leader of the RW and a hardworking mother. My husband and I have loved our daughter, our only Mercy, from when she was born a premature. I cannot believe that my husband did this thing you are accusing him of. Besides, our daughter is here and she denies having said any of what this girl is claiming. Chief, I wonder who in this village is behind this, who is setting up this poor girl against my family, who wants to see us go down. Is it because of jealous? Is it because of my position in the RW, or perhaps because my family is perfect ...?'

Chipo stares at Mother, not believing her evilness in sacrificing her own child like this. With begging eyes, she looks at Mercy, who is sitting on the ground next to Mother and Tete and still looking calm, praying that her friend puts and end this charade.

After whispering with his close elders, Chief Kamutsi calls for Mercy, who wipes away tears from her eyes and takes to her feet.

'My daughter,' Chief Kamutsi says, 'you are the only person here that can lead this court to the truth, so do not be afraid. You must know that this court is fully behind you my daughter, so please tell us what happened on the day in question.'

'Thank you, chief,' Mercy says with some hesitation. 'I have no reason to lie to you or to hide anything. The truth is that I was not raped by anyone, not by *baba* or by any other man. As you all know, Chipo is my good friend, my best friend. She and I were supposed to go to the village centre, but when she came by our home she found me sleeping in my hut. I told her that I was not feeling well and could no longer go with her, so she went alone. It was only when she came back in the evening that she started asking me questions which I was uncomfortable with. She suggested to me that *baba* had to do with my being ill, which I knew was not true, but because I wanted to punish *baba* I lied to her that he raped me. Chief, the truth is that my father did nothing like that. What he did was that he beat me up when he discovered that I had a boyfriend, Freedom, from Village Six, that I planned to meet him at the village centre. It is because of my love for Freedom and of his beating me and barring me from going to the centre that I was angry with him. Forgive me please, I did not mean to cause any trouble...'

The court is filled with gasps, followed by a great silence. Chief Kamutsi is short of words, he doesn't know how to proceed. He leans forward on his staff, looks into

Mercy's eyes and says, 'My daughter, are you sure of what you are saying, the implications of it?'

'Yes, chief, I am sure,' she says, tears rolling down her cheeks once again.

'Then, if you are so sure, why is it that your father left the village for a whole month, only to come back in the state that he is now?'

'Chief, I think *mama* has already answered that question. Where *baba* was and why it took him so long to come back to the house, I think that is for him to answer.' She looks at Father, and he looks at her briefly before dropping his eyes to the ground. 'He hurt me so much when he beat me. I think that he felt guilty because he had never touched me before,' she says.

Chief Kamutsi is silent for a while. He signals for Mercy to sit down.

Chipo is in tears. She cannot believe what she just heard, she worries about how this is going to affect her friendship with Mercy, what she will say to her and how she will look Father in the eyes again. She blames herself for being too forward.

Chief Kamutsi and the elders retreat into an inner room to deliberate, leaving the court in commotion as people try to make sense of what just happened, arguing about what action the elders and Chief Kamutsi should take.

When he comes back, slowly like before, Chief Kamutsi has a decision. 'It is unfortunate my people that we have subjected our brother to this humiliation all because of a lie, a stupid lie,' he says after taking a lot of time settling down, 'so, because of the time wasted, I hereby charge that Petros and Mangwiro have a week to each pay a goat to the chief's court as punishment for the despicable actions of their daughters. The court completely discharges and exonerates Petros. He is free to go.'

With this, Chief Kamutsi takes to his feet and slowly disappears into his room, through the arch. Privately, he is relieved that Father has been found not guilty, but his kidneys wonder whether the allegations could be true.

On the way home, Mercy, Mother and Tete lead the way. Father walks behind them, slowly.

When they arrive, Mercy cries her heart out. She locks herself up in her hut for many days, only getting out to take a bath and to go to school, and once to accompany Tete to catch the bus back to the city.

For a long time, Freedom doesn't want anything to do with her. Chipo also stays away. Mercy is not bothered by all of this, she is not in the mood for friendship and does not at all regret her decision to let Father go. Her friends will learn to live with it. After all, Mother was right, some people in the village would have been happy to see Father go to jail. She could not gift that to them. Besides, Father has since been good, kinder. He now frequents Mother's church, like he has truly turned a new leaf.

Mercy spends her time cleaning Reverend Mbudzi's house, which is near the school. His lovely wife and child are happy to have her, so she spends a lot of her time there or buried in her books. The year is soon coming to a close and next year will be important for her. She has to get the 5 O Levels, at all cost.

It is like this, with things going just fine since the incident with Father two months ago, that Mercy and Mother visit the clinic after she has missed school for most of the week due to stomach pains and a headache which are messing up with her studies. Mother ascribes this to the witches of the village who do not want her to prosper, and to the women who are fighting to dethrone her from the RW leadership.

When they arrive at the clinic, Nurse Mupunga asks them to skip the line and come straight in. She too is a member of Mother's church, who would benefit from her benevolence. After some preliminary checks, she takes a sample of Mercy's urine and dips a piece of paper into it. When she looks at it again she is less smiling. 'Mai Mercy,' she says, 'is your daughter sexually active?'

'What do you mean?' Mercy and Mother speak at the same time, with alarm.

'Well, Mercy here is pregnant,' she continues, attempting a smile.

'No, no, no, please God, no,' Mother cries.

Mercy storms out of the room and walks towards the village centre like one who has lost their mind. Mother follows right behind her, walking and running and wiping her eyes, trying to catch-up with her daughter who is completely crashed.

Four

Ruby's clinic

Mother's assurance does not make her feel any better. It makes her more nervous about what lies ahead, whether or not this Ruby will be of any help to her. She knows very well that there is no other way, that what has to be done has to be. After all, who can withstand the load of bringing up a child who is also their sibling, whose grandfather is also their father?

In the dead of the night, Father leads the way as they negotiate the narrow footpath that goes into the valley, careful not to step onto the tails of live snakes since the moon is not there tonight. Mercy and Mother follow behind, quietly, the long grass along the sides of the path swishing against their legs. No-one else is up at this hour except for the hyenas, the owls and the witches. From a distance a hyena's cry cuts through the silence, that eerie sound from the ugly creature whose hunting antics border between fear and intimidation. The villagers believe that the hyena cries only when it is hungry, otherwise when it is full it laughs; the following day they would wake up to missing chickens and goats.

None of them says nothing as they slowly descend into Mupfurati and are treated to a chorus of big and small frogs shouting and answering each other like a trained choir. Mupfurati is full and not at all easy to cross, thanks to the gods who delivered the rains of recent weeks. Father is first to take off his battered shoes and hang them around his neck, quietly. Mercy and Mother do the same, then the three of them hold hands and carefully step into the angry waters one leg at a time. At first the water is up to their knees, so they drag their feet against the bottom of the river and feel the power of the surging waters threatening to sweep them away. A few steps and the water is up to their waist, and chest, lifting up Mother's dress and colourful petticoat and filling up the pockets of Father's pants.

On the other side, they quietly slip back into their shoes, Mercy and Mother twisting their dresses to drain the water. They resume their journey, finding themselves on the wider path that runs parallel to the gravel road used by motorists and the mostly absent public transport. They are on it for a good long walk before they branch off towards Village Thirteen, going along the mountain range and plunging into Ruby's small and isolated compound. It has only two huts, and light is emanating from a tiny opening below the thatch of one of these. Mercy's heart is pounding like *bira* drums being beat by a drunk woman. She clings on to Mother as they step into the yard, who holds her hand firmly without saying a word.

Father knocks on the door of the hut and waits for a response.

'The door is open,' a tiny voice comes from inside. It sounds like that of a young girl.

Father pushes the door inside and steps in.

He puts his hands together in the manner of men.

Mother and Mercy follow behind and sit on the same side as Father. The woman inside is indeed much younger than Mercy pictured in her head. She is sitting on her folded legs by the fire, facing the direction Mercy and her parents are sitting. On the dying fire, in the middle of the hut, are three dirty pots simmering with something which immediately makes Mercy want to vomit because of its smell. She has no idea what it is.

A paraffin lamp is hung against the wall.

'Mai Mercy,' Ruby says with a big smile. 'I knew you would come, and you have done the right thing my friend, you have come to the right place.' She talks fast, the words pouring out of her like water out of a pressured pump, much like Mapudege twisting a simple story and not wanting to give her victims a chance to think.

Mother cups her hands in greeting. She introduces Mercy, who is the only one Ruby has never met before. 'You know why we are here,' she says, 'and we do not want to waste any time, lest the sun is up on us before we are back in our beds. We decided to come here because we trust you, you are professional and mature.'

'I will not disappoint you my friend, so don't worry at all. All your problems are over,' Ruby says, then she looks directly at Mercy as if searching for her eyes.

'Let's get it done and over with,' Father says.

'This is the right thing, Mercy,' Mother says, squeezing Mercy's hand with her thumb in order to reassure her. 'You know we can't have this baby. We have come a long way. Where we are going is much closer, then we all get our lives back.'

Mercy nods her head in agreement. All she wants now is to get rid of this thing, but she is afraid. Afraid of the procedure itself and afraid of the burden that she will have to carry after it is done. Will she tell her future husband about it? What would Freedom think if he were to know about it? The trouble though, is that the alternative is not at all palatable. How would she face the people back in the village? Chipo and Freedom and the other children at school? She has to do it. Like Father said, she has to get it done and over with.

'The girl will lie on her back right there,' Ruby says as she points towards a thick plastic covered with a small brown blanket, 'but she will have to drink each of these portions first, all, one after the other. This will ensure that it becomes loose and weak, then we will do what else needs to be done.'

Mercy looks at the three pots with eyes popping out, and asks, 'All of this?'

Ruby nods her head.

Mercy looks at the pots again. She doesn't understand how it would be possible to empty all of that garbage into her tiny stomach given the sheer size of the pots and the smell.

'You cannot stop once you begin. Here, take this cup,' Ruby says and hands her a blue plastic cup. It is huge.

Mercy grabs the cup with shivering hands and dips into the first pot. She scoops one, closes her eyes and offloads it into her stomach in large gulps. It is bitter. She scoops another and does the same, Father and Mother looking intently at her, their eyes following the downward and upward movement of the cup and nodding their heads. In a few minutes, she is done with the first pot and now feels full, like the liquid is coming up to her throat, like she is drowning in it. Her stomach feels hard, so she hesitates to go into the next pot.

'All the way my girl,' Ruby says, 'otherwise this won't work. This, my friend, is the price of sleeping around ...'

Mercy dips into the second pot and takes in two straight cups, bringing this to the halfway mark, but she really can't go any further. She struggles to breathe or talk.

'Don't stop, Mercy darling,' Mother says. 'You are almost there. Just this little bit and you are done.'

Mercy scoops one more cup and holds it halfway between the pot and her mouth. She doesn't have any more space to put it. She looks at Father, then at Mother and Ruby, with begging eyes, as if to say 'please tell me to stop.' Mother nods her head for encouragement. Mercy brings the cup close to her mouth and pauses. There is an unravelling inside her tummy, like of one who has spent the whole day eating wild guavas along the banks of Mupfurati. She feels it rise up her throat. She throws out all that she took with great ferocity, as if she would throw out even her insides.

Mother kneels next to her and presses between her shoulders on the back. Mercy holds her tummy as her intestines make huge somersaults.

'What do we do now?' Mother asks Ruby. 'Will this still work?'

'Well, not without the medicine having been absorbed into the body,' Ruby says. 'I spent the whole day preparing this for her. Now that she has thrown up everything, it means that we have to start afresh.'

'Afresh!' Mercy exclaims in a tired voice, breathing fast and furious. Sweat trickles down her face.

'There is no other way,' Ruby says.

Father gets up to his feet and paces around the small hut, scratching his head and saying nothing. Mother pleads with Mercy to take the remaining liquid and finish the job. Mercy is too tired to agree or disagree. She just sits there, staring at the pots like a zombie.

'Finish it please my daughter,' Mother says in a cracking voice. 'We can't come all this way for nothing.'

'This is now just half of the required amount, so not sure if it still works,' Ruby says.

'What are you saying now, Ruby? That we quit?' Mother asks.

'We can try, but now there is no guarantee.'

'Please.'

'Does she still want to carry on?' Ruby asks, lifting up Mercy's head by the chin and handing her a clean cup.

Mercy silently dips into the pot again. She is done in a few scoops and moves on to the third. By the time she is done there is war inside her tummy, but she ignores it. She battles to suppress the urge to vomit it all out again.

'Well done my daughter,' Mother says, rubbing her shoulder.

'Now we have to try and release it,' says Ruby, looking at Mercy. 'Lie on the blanket. Trust me.'

Father observes Mercy as she lies on the blanket on her back and Ruby positions her legs like one who is about to give birth to a set of twins. He cannot bring himself to look again, so he walks out of the hut and sits on a log of wood a stone's throw away, praying to his ancestors.

Meanwhile, Mercy is tired. She lies there like a dead person, her eyes closed. She feels Ruby's fingers stroking and parting, then making circles just inside her. It hurts. In a few minutes, she feels the tip of Ruby's hand inside. She groans.

Mother sits there, praying in her heart. She asks God to deliver her from this misery and to forgive her sin. Never again will she subject her conscience to this torture. Never again will she agree to anything like this. She raises her eyebrows as Ruby draws out a smooth hooked wire from the edge of the sooty, thatched roof.

Mercy keeps her eyes closed.

She screams when the wire moves up inside her, guided by Ruby's fingers. She feels like she is going to pee.

Father can hear her cries from where he is, so he moves a little further away.

The wire deep inside her, Mercy feels it turn, like Ruby is trying to hook something. She cries like a woman in labour, Mother pinning her to the ground by the arms. She feels Ruby tag at something inside of her and pull.

'Stop! Stop!' she cries in pain.

Ruby doesn't stop. She keeps tagging and pulling until Mercy's cry is unbearable. She puts her fingers inside and turns the wire, and when she pulls it out a gush of blood follows, messing up her hand and the blanket. 'Oh no!' she exclaims, and sighs. 'This is not working.'

'Please try, Ruby darling,' Mother begs her. She can't believe it, that they could have come all this way for nothing.

'No, Mai Mercy, she is losing too much blood. We will lose her if we continue. It's her fault. She should have taken all the medicine. Then it would have been much easier.'

Mother sits there sobbing, not just for herself, but also for her daughter.

Mercy stays on the floor writhing with pain.

Father comes back inside, after the crying has stopped. He looks at Mother, then at Ruby and Mercy. None of them says a word, so he asks, 'Success?'

Ruby and Mother shake their heads, slowly.

He looks at Mercy, then looks away. He sits on the small bench in the hut and puts his head between his knees.

Helpless, Mercy, Mother and Father stay in the hut a few more minutes, and when they finally leave the compound it is at the break of dawn. Mother and Father take turns to carry Mercy on their backs like a child. She is weak.

Five

That which has horns

She is sitting on a wooden chair in the back of the classroom, with Freedom and Chipo. Lovemore is not in today, his father failed to pay his tuition fees, prompting the headmaster to bar him and many other children from the classrooms. VaMusungwa goes from class to class calling out the children's names and asking them to leave the school premises. Freedom is sitting next to her, his chair facing the opposite direction of the chalkboard. He does most of the talking as Chipo and the other children giggle to his lurid jokes. The girls are especially impressed with his wit. The boy that grew up in the city, he thinks that they all like him. It gives him lots of wings.

Mercy does not laugh or smile. She is in a world she can only share with mothers, not with these toddlers who have no idea what it means to be with child. She ignores the periodic tightening and loosening inside her belly, which is as if the baby is pinching and letting go of her womb at will. Oftentimes, she is short of breath, but nobody notices. No-one at the school knows about what's growing inside of her, or of the bag of painkillers that is kept hidden inside her school bag. No-one in the village either, except for Nurse Mupunga who Mother has since taken care of by making her deputy of the RW. Mother knows that she will never say a word to anyone. She has it all figured out.

Mercy's expanding abdomen bothers her. It is not yet hugely visible, partly because of it being her first and partly because she has her tummy bound underneath the clothes with Mother's plastic belt. She only lets loose of it during the night when she goes to sleep. To her friends, she is just as always, but on the inside, she worries about how all this will pan out for her. After all, as the elders say, 'that which has horns cannot be wrapped up in paper,' she knows that one day she will have to face up to her situation. The thought of it makes her sick. She hopes, however, that it will never come to that, that she will be able to hide this thing to the very end. Mother assured her that she has a good plan of disposing of the unwanted thing before it can see the light of day. It was her idea to bind the tummy and so far, it has worked just as planned, she has no reason to not trust her.

'What's bothering you?' Freedom asks, lowering his voice and looking at Mercy straight in the eye.

She attempts a smile, unconvincingly, to mask her distress.

'Yes, Mercy, what is it? You behave so strange these days,' Chipo agrees.

Mercy attempts yet another smile. She looks away, across the room, then down at the floor. 'Why won't you people leave me alone?' she finally says, lifting up her head and blinking her eyes many times. 'I am not loud, that's all, that doesn't make me a miserable person. We all have something to worry about, including you…'

'You're right,' says Freedom in a more serious tone, yet in jest, 'which is why you need to loosen up, otherwise you will grow old before I, your man, is even ready to get married.. '

'Precisely,' agrees Chipo.

'Okay. Maybe you two need to tickle me so I can be happy,' Mercy says, with a genuine smile. Freedom takes it literally, so he tries to tickle her. She jumps up to her feet and runs away from him, he in pursuit. 'Are you crazy? Leave me alone,' she says, giggling and pushing chairs and desks to prevent Freedom from getting to her.

The other children whistle and shout in excitement, and in no time the classroom is now like the village beerhall on a Saturday night. They raise their voices and bang the desks, inviting VaMusungwa's unwanted attention. They are too caught up to notice him stand by the open door, swinging a fan-belt in his right hand, the left one tucked into the pocket of his tight trousers. Those that see him first quietly take to their seats, waiting for the others to get the signal before they too abruptly knock down some chairs as they run back to their desks. Then there is dead silence.

Freedom and Mercy freeze where they are, in the middle of the room and far away from their desks, totally guilty. Mercy's breathing is high, but so is everyone else's. Feeling very light, she slumps onto the cement floor on her butt.

'Get up!' VaMusungwa's stern voice bellows across the room the majority of whose windows are either broken or have no glass at all. It doesn't occur to him that there could be anything wrong with her.

'Has it sunk into your thick skulls that you are now the senior class of this school?' he continues. 'What example are you setting for the juniors? Freedom. Mercy. You disappoint me and I have no choice but to make a good example of you.'

Mercy remains on the floor, battling to stabilise her breathing. She can feel the weight of her head. Feeling dizzy, she sees the stars and can barely hear Freedom's voice.

'We are sorry, sir,' Freedom says, cupping his hands together in a begging manner, his head tilted to the left.

'Sorry, huh?' says VaMusungwa. 'Since when has sorry been good enough to pay a debt? Your parents sell their crops and herds to get you to school, and all you have to repay them with is 'sorry'? Why do you people defecate on the exact same place where you eat? No, no, no. It won't be just to let you go like that, I would have failed to do my job. I have to show your friends a good example of what not to do. That is the only language you morons can understand.'

His hands itching to get a cracking at the duo, VaMusungwa walks towards them. Freedom backpedals to the back of the room until he is against the wall, timid. Mercy makes no reaction. The other children watch in silence, like they are watching one of the productions normally performed in the open air theatre at the village centre.

'I will start with you,' VaMusungwa says to Mercy, clenching and baring his teeth like a menacing dog. 'Ladies first,' he says, laughing sarcastically.

Mercy struggles to her feet, the chairs and desks spinning all around her, VaMusungwa's voice sounding to her like someone speaking into an empty well hundreds of meters deep. All she can hear are sounds and echoes. She stands there, like a deer caught in the dazzling lights of a new car, until she feels her eardrum shut as VaMusungwa's huge hand falls against her face. She falls to the ground on her side. He follows up with three consecutive lashes against her behind, her thin dress lifting with each strike. He is about to dish her a fourth when he stops mid-air. Something is not right. Mercy is not her usual self. On another day, she would have run around the room begging for mercy and would have cried at the top of her voice so as to be let go. She does none of that.

He drops the belt to the ground, kneels next to her and shakes her by the shoulder. There is no response. He panics. 'Mercy. Mercy!' he calls, pressing two fingers against her neck for a pulse, then against her wrist.

No response.

He bolts out of the classroom.

When he comes back in the company of two female teachers, there is total commotion.

'She is breathing,' one of them says, after feeling her pulse.

'We should call the ambulance,' says the other. She runs out towards the administration block.

The children now sing and dance in protest, overturning the chairs and tables in the room. '*We told you, and now you have killed her. Yes, it's you who has killed her. We told you so but you thought you were a god. You have killed her, yes you have killed her*,' they sing with lots of anger, pointing their fingers at VaMusungwa who is now like a live chicken bathed in hot water, sweat pouring down his face. The noise quickly attracts the attention of the other school children who in no time surround the classroom block and peep through the broken windows to get a glimpse of the happenings.

When the teacher who went to call the ambulance comes back, the rest of the teaching staff is now in the room. 'We can't wait for the ambulance,' she says. 'We have to take her to the clinic. The driver is on his way.'

'Take her shoes off,' one of the teachers suggests.

Another suggests that they loosen her collar as he fans her with an open book. 'Clear up, clear up, give her some air,' he says as he pushes back the school children with his outstretched arms. The children leave the classroom and assemble outside, singing and dancing and joined by the rest of the school. Freedom does not sing with them. He and Chipo remain in the classroom in a state of shock, huddling together in fear.

Soon, the school truck arrives and they bundle Mercy into the open back cabin, a few of the teachers and her two friends jumping in with her before the driver takes off to the clinic, which is not far. VaMusungwa locks himself up in his office as the other teachers try to calm the protesting children who are now throwing stones, breaking the remaining windows of the classrooms. Eventually, the teachers let them go for the day. The children go to their homes talking about the incident, itching to tell their parents all about it. Many of them are happy that, for once, VaMusungwa has made a blunder that could hurt him. They don't like him at all. 'He killed her,' that they all agree.

Mercy is rushed into an inner room at the clinic, which has two beds which are both unoccupied. The two nurses on duty attend to her in the presence of her two friends and a female teacher.

'What happened?' Nurse Mupunga asks.

'She just collapsed,' the female teacher says, casting a quick glance at Freedom in a manner designed to buy his loyalty.

He refuses to be silenced. 'Not true,' he says. 'It was VaMusungwa. He beat her up with a fan belt until she fainted.'

'You mean to tell me that the headmaster did this?' Nurse Mupunga asks as she looks at the teacher and shakes her head.

'Of course,' charges Freedom, 'but that is not new. We get this treatment every day, but this time the old man is going to pay for it.'

'Who are you?' Nurse Mupunga asks Freedom. 'Are you related to her?'

'No.'

'He is a friend,' Chipo quickly intervenes, but Nurse Mupunga does not pay attention, she was not expecting a response.

'She will be fine,' she says. 'The doctor will be here soon.'

Freedom and Chipo wait outside the room for some time before the doctor shows up on one of the two district ambulances. When she arrives, Mercy has now regained consciousness and is sitting on the bed, Mother by her side.

When Mother arrived a while ago, she made sure to register her anger against the teachers for mistreating her child, and vowed to deal with VaMusungwa when this is all over. Now, she is sitting in the room uncomfortably. She and Nurse Mupunga keep glancing at each other, knowingly.

The doctor looks at the nurse's notes and has a few words with Mother and the nurses, then asks Mercy to lie down on the neatly done bed, on her back. Mother does not like it. There is stirring inside her tummy and her heart is pounding hard. She watches as the doctor examines her eyes and ears and touches her feet. She cringes when she starts pressing on the tummy and unpins the front buttons of her blouse, revealing the pink plastic belt underneath. Very wide. She loosens it and the tummy pops out a bit. She looks at Mercy, who is now in tears. 'Can I have a word with the mother and the girl, alone,' she commands.

The nurses and the teacher leave the room.

'Please get up, and take a seat,' says the doctor as she takes Mercy by the hand and pulls a chair for Mother. She sits on the other chair and smiles.

'What is it?' Mother asks, knowing very well that the cat is out of bag. She tries to be strong. She at least has to pretend like she doesn't know anything.

'Are you feeling okay, Mercy?' the doctor asks.

She nods her head as the tears pour down her face one more time. She has shed more tears in the past three months than she has done her entire life. There just doesn't seem to be an end to her troubles.

The doctor looks up at Mother with a more serious face. 'I am sorry to disappoint you mother, but your daughter is pregnant. She was hiding it by binding her belly,' she says.

Mother knew that this was coming, but she does not know what to say when the words finally hit her. She simply looks down and shakes her head. It's game over, she thinks.

'It's nothing to worry about, mother. Teenage pregnancy is something we are dealing with all over the country. What your daughter now needs is to be loved and looked after. It is not the end of the world.'

The doctor smiles, then asks the deadly question, 'Who is the father of the child?'

Mercy hides her face between her hands and knees, hurt and angry and helpless. She shakes her head furiously.

The doctor wraps her right arm around her shoulder. 'I think she might open up to a counsellor,' she says to Mother, then takes to her feet, dangling her stethoscope in her hand. She goes out to talk to the nurses and the teacher who all express shock at the news.

'She is one of our best students,' says the teacher. 'What a shame!'

When the teacher walks away, she is shaking her head. She is glad that the girl is still alive and that after all, it was not VaMusungwa's beating that caused her to be in that condition. She is still trying to come to terms with the news when the other teachers, together with Chipo and Freedom, run to meet her. 'She is pregnant,' she says before they ask, to everyone's astonishment.

'What!' Freedom exclaims. He doesn't understand how. He hasn't touched her at all.

'Is it yours, Freedom?' asks Chipo. The teachers all turn to look at him, but he ignores them.

'How long?' he asks.

'Three months.'

Chipo's brains are sent on a sprint. She quickly works out that it was just over three months ago, when Mercy claimed that she was raped by her father, when she was made a complete fool at Chief Kamutsi's compound a few weeks later. She forgave her then, but not anymore, not with this news. It changes everything.

Freedom too is angry. He leaves in a huff, cursing the air as he goes.

Chipo knows it is all over between her two friends and she wonders what is going to happen now, whether this is the time that she will be vindicated. She too doesn't wait for Mercy and Mother; she leaves in a hurried manner to break the news to Mangwiro.

When Mercy and Mother get home, Father is still away with the cattle. It is just before sunset and he has no idea what is happening around him.

They find Mapudege waiting for them, sitting by the kitchen door, when they walk into the compound like people who have lost the will to live. They don't talk to each other or to anyone. Mercy heads straight on to her hut, her school bag weighing on her back as if full of sand, her mind frozen. She doesn't know whether she is alive or dead. She can't feel herself.

'Mai Mercy, my friend,' Mapudege says, 'thank God you are here. We have to organise the RW so we can have a demonstration at that shameless monkey's school. Who does he think he is, that we are all his wives and children, huh? Mai Mercy, please tell me that you beat up that monkey-head or I will go do it myself. Who beats up a child like that, a girl for that matter? Where does he even touch …?'

Mother does not respond. She doesn't want to. She knows the news will be all over the village come tomorrow morning and she will have nowhere to hide. She knows that all Mapudege wants is something with which to paint the village, that tomorrow she will have all she needs to do precisely that.

Mapudege follows Mother around the yard as she unpins her washing from the line and takes it into her bedroom hut.

'What's wrong with you, Mai Mercy?' Mapudege says as she waits by the door of the hut. 'Why do you ignore me as if I am the one who told that stupid headmaster to beat up your child? All I am trying to do here is help, but you people do not appreciate it at all …'

Mother still does not say a word. She opens the kitchen door and starts preparing a fire. It takes her longer than usual to get this up and going.

Meanwhile, Mapudege is sitting on the cement bench inside the hut, talking to herself. She wonders what it could be that's making Mother to be so mean as to give her such a cold shoulder. It is unlike her. There must be something wrong somewhere and she is not going to leave before she gets all the juicy bits out.

She decides to go talk to Mercy, so she walks to her hut.

Without knocking, she pushes the door inside. '*Maihweee?*' she cries in a loud voice, which startles Mother. 'Mai Mercy. Mai Mercy!' she calls in a serious, half-crying voice.

Mother panics. She runs to the hut.

Mapudege is now by the door, wailing.

'What is it?' Mother asks as she pushes her aside and enters the room. She comes face to face with Mercy, lying on the floor in her uniform, just by the door, her mouth frothing and her face against the floor. Her bag lies open and the books and pens strewn all over the place. She is not moving.

'Mercy. Mercy!' Mother shouts as she turns her around to reveal her turned-over eyes. '*Maihweee!*' she cries. She shakes her and listens to her heartbeat. There is a weak response. 'Mercy my daughter, please do not leave me like this, please,' she cries.

'Mother,' Mercy finally says in a faint, fading voice, 'I am sorry.' The voice dies away and she drops her head.

'She talked,' Mother calls out. She runs out of the house and comes face to face with a few other people rushing into the yard. They have heard of Mapudege's cry and think that someone has died. They keep asking, 'who is it, who is it?' Mapudege explains that she was the first one to see Mercy in that state, that had it not been because of her Mercy would have been dead by now. Now, she is only crying to God so he can save her.

It is dark when Father arrives from the cattle pens. The villagers have already rushed Mercy back to the clinic in a scotch-cart and VaMusungwa has provided the school truck which took her to the district hospital. When Father rushes over to the clinic, the nurse explains to him that Mercy most likely overdosed on painkillers, that her survival will depend on how quickly the driver gets her to the district hospital.

Six

Fresh air

She has been in the hospital for a week and Mother and Father have been with her all the time, except during the night when they sleep in shop verandas at the district market, together with vendors who come to sell their excess produce there. Mother wishes she could just stay at the hospital forever. She dreads going back to the village. Father spends most of his time milling around the market, walking up and down, except for yesterday when he went to Dorowera for an audience with the great man there.

In the morning, when he arrives back at the hospital, Father finds Tete sitting with Mother and Mercy on the veranda of the hospital's main wing, basking in the morning sunshine. Mercy is now a lot better, although she remains subdued. Now she can eat and bath on her own. The doctor says that she is out of the woods but needs counselling, that her illness is now more of the mind than of the flesh.

'Welcome, brother,' Tete says.

'Thank you, Tari, and welcome,' Father replies. 'Thank you for coming.' He sits quietly on the wooden bench there, alongside a few other people.

'Are you coming from the village?'

'No.'

'Mai Mercy said you left yesterday. I thought you would have gone to the village?'

'I went to see a friend.'

'Leaving your wife and daughter without saying where you were going?'

'Tari, why do you terrorise me? It was only for a day. Mercy is better now, can't you see?'

'Alright then, I will leave you alone, but I am not leaving without her. I will take Mercy with me to the city.'

'But she has school and exams ...'

'Let her go, *baba*,' Mother intervenes. 'It is for the best. She can always write her exams next year.'

'Well, if you say so.'

Tete's offer is a gift from the heavens. Now Mother won't have to worry about explaining to Mapudege and the village women where Mercy's pregnancy came from. But her position at the RW is now at risk. She knows that the women will not let her continue in that capacity after her daughter's disgrace, it is not acceptable that the daughter of the chair of the RW be such a bad example. She will have to relinquish her position, but she will not go without a fight. After all, the Mbudzis like her, so they will not just let her go, unless if their hearts have also now been turned against her because of this.

'I have already spoken to the nurses and they have agreed that if the doctor lets her go today, I can take her with me right away,' explains Tete. 'I will get her into a good community college that is more supportive.'

Father agrees. He springs up to his feet and excuses himself. He walks down the long corridor, whistling to himself.

Tete grabs the opportunity to engage Mercy one more time. 'Mercy, darling,' she says, 'you need to talk to me. I am your aunt, you know? I deserve to be told the truth about these kinds of matters. You know, I will support you no matter what.'

Mercy looks at her but says nothing. She looks at Mother and Mother looks away.

Tete continues, 'I need you to tell me who the father of this child is. It is important that we know this. Besides, the father also deserves to know. Tell me, niece, who is it?'

Mercy shakes her head. 'I don't know,' she says.

Tete does not believe her. She has always known Mercy to be intelligent. 'No, Mercy, that is impossible. Were you involved with more than one man?'

She nods her head.

'Are you sure, darling? I don't want to open old wounds but you know the drama of three months ago, at Chief Kamutsi's court, does this have anything to do with that?'

Mercy is surprised by herself. She is calm and collected. 'No,' she says.

Tete sighs. 'Alright then, I believe you. But you need to figure out who is responsible, and you don't have much time.'

Mercy nods her head.

'Good.'

Mother breathes a sigh of relief, but she isn't sure how long Mercy will hold on, how long she will keep this to herself, especially when she's living in the city with Tete. She also worries about what will become of the child when it is born, how Mercy and Father and she will live with that knowledge for the rest of their lives. But for now, she is happy to cross that bridge when she comes to it. She will make a plan.

The villagers watch as the four make their way up the hill from the village centre, in a single file. They look at them with curious eyes, as if trying to read their minds. The expectation was that there was going to be a fracas, as rumour has it that the child is Father's. Mother should not be taking it easy like this, she should be threatening to leave Father, to go back to her parents' home in Village Thirteen. It boggles the mind that this is not happening.

When they get home, Mercy hastily packs her bags and leaves without saying goodbye to Chipo or Freedom. Not that they expected her to say anything anyway, since they are still unhappy with how she lied to them.

Father and Mother accompany Tete and Mercy to the village centre, where they take the bus, and when they are returning from there they are met on the way with one of Chief Kamutsi's messengers who summons them to the chief's homestead.

They find Chief Kamutsi sitting outside, in the compound, with his two sons. 'Is that you, Petros?' he asks, rhetorically.

'Yes, chief, it is I.'

Mother cups her hands in greeting and unwinds the shawl which she has wound around her waist, to sit on in the shade.

'Please take a seat,' invites Chief Kamutsi.

Father sits on three stacked bricks, close to Mother who sits on the shawl which she spreads on the ground. Father puts his hands together in greeting as Mother cups her hands one more time. Chief Kamutsi's sons and the messenger do the same as Chief Kamutsi continues to hold and support his weight against his staff, the tip of which is pressed hard into the sand. He leans forwards and speaks in a hoarse voice.

'The reason why I called for you, Petros, I think you know it,' he says. 'A few months ago we were here, in the court over there, and we were presiding over the case of your daughter. You know everything that happened then, and you yourself, together with Mangwiro, parted with some beasts as punishment. Now, the village is abuzz with the same story. What we neglected to ask then, my son, was whether your daughter was seeing someone. Not that it would have been any problem to us, you know what I mean, but the problem that we have today is that the question is being asked again, whether you have anything to do with this, your daughter's pregnancy?'

When he pauses, Father again puts his hands together and says, 'Chief, you are like a father to me, one I have the utmost respect for. Your father and my grandfather were great friends, so were you and my late father. Please indulge me a little, so I can reason with you. Chief, why would a father like me rape his own daughter, his only daughter for that matter, especially when he has a whole wife like this, who is admired by many people? Why would a snake kill that which it does not eat? Do I look to you like one who could do something like that? Oh chief, why do the people of this village hate my family so much as to wish us something so bad?'

'So, you are denying it again Petros, just like your daughter then? Are you sure, Petros, that when it comes this child will not bear your resemblance, that it will not have your blood flowing in its veins? You know my son, that would be a big problem for us, a terrible thing to say the least. We don't want to anger the gods and end up with calamity.'

Father coughs and says, 'You have my word, chief. Let the gods be my witness, let them strike me dead if I lie. Let the child come and prove all these running-mouths wrong. If the child bears any resemblance with me, which I doubt it will, it would only be due to the fact that Mercy is my daughter. Nothing else.'

'If you say so, Petros. But be warned, lies and immorality have a habit of choking their bearer. One can only reap that which they sow. If you sow steak, you will certainly reap maggots.'

With these words, Chief Kamutsi takes to his feet and walks away. He disappears into one of the many huts in the compound.

They go back home relieved, but now quarrel about something else.

'Where were you last night?' Mother asks several times before getting a response.

'Nowhere important,' Father finally replies.

'Don't lie to me. I know it when you are not telling the truth.'

'Well, if you know as you say, then you ought to also know that I was just around the market.'

'Around the market?'

'Yes.'

'So where did you sleep, as I do not remember seeing you at the end of the day?'

'Why does that matter, Mai Mercy? One should just have a little trust in their own husband, you know.'

'A little trust, huh?' Mother asks, angrily. 'You are the reason why we are in this mess. Can you look me in the eye and tell me you did not go to Dorowera?'

Father looks away, then says, 'Mai Mercy, you know I had to see him. Things are now complicated as you know. We cannot just wait and see what happens. Someone needed to do something. And it worked. See, now Tari has come and solved the problem.'

'Why do you still trust that idiot anyway? Has our life really got any better? Has the opposite not happened? My husband, you need to wake up and stop behaving like a child before we become the laughing stock of the village.'

With these words, Mother walks faster, ahead of him.

He follows behind and shouts after her, 'Why do you want to put it all on me? That is not fair, Mai Mercy. Did your church-people help anyway? Answer me, woman. Nonsense! …'

Mercy feels a little better as the bus drifts away from the village. Until now she did not realise how much she longed to be away from there, away from Chipo and Freedom and Mother and Father. She did not realise how much seeing them over and again choked the life out of her, how much it embedded into her soul the guilt and the shame, robbing her of the happiness. Now she can focus on delivering her baby and making a new life in the city. Everything will now be fine.

She has a new hope.

In Mutare, they are met at the bus station with Biggie, who Tete introduces. 'He is a friend of mine,' she says.

'Hello there,' Biggie says as he extends his arm for a handshake.

'Hello,' Mercy says, allowing him to take her hand.

'She is my niece, the one I told you about,' continues Tete. 'She will stay with us.'

'Happy to meet you, Mercy.'

He holds her hand a little longer than she expected. It feels strong and rough. He looks much younger than Tete.

She smiles, shyly, and pulls her hand back, but she does not stop looking at his masculine body, the wide chest and huge arms protruding through the open vest which is too small for his size. She has never seen a young man as strong and built as he is. She watches him kiss Tete on the cheek and lift up the two big bags into the boot of the waiting taxi in one go. She sits in the front passenger seat as Biggie and Tete sit in the back.

Home is not too far away from the CBD. It is a decent area with houses neatly arranged and packed into rows and columns, with lots of people milling around the streets and wandering aimlessly. A few young boys are kicking about a plastic ball in a game of football right in the middle of the tarred road, goalposts being little stones on either side of the road and one of the teams having stripped off their shirts.

The taxi pulls outside the house at the corner, at the end of the street, which has a washed-out blue paint and is the only blue in the street, the others being mainly cream or unpainted. The low perimeter fence around the house is broken in several places although the gate, which is made of steel bars, is still intact.

Tete unlocks the gate and Biggie grabs the bags from the boot of the car. Mercy follows behind the pair into the house of which entrance is in the back.

'Hey,' the driver of the taxi honks the horn of car. 'My money!'

'Ah, sorry,' says Tete, laughing. 'I had completely forgotten.' She looks inside her purse and pulls out a bundle of notes. 'This should be it.'

'Thanks, madam,' the driver says, beaming. 'Call me anytime and I will come running.' He drives away, slowly, disrupting the kids' football game.

Inside, the house is beautifully done. There are two bedrooms, one of which is used by Tete. The spare bedroom has a single bed and is full of unwashed clothes and building items stacked in the corners. The clothes are so many that Mercy wonders how one could have so much, about how many people these could clothe for years back in the village.

'Feel at home,' Tete says. 'Biggie will prepare your room.'

'Thank you, aunty. Your house is very nice; you should have come for me earlier.'

'Not with that father of yours. He loves you too much He wouldn't let me. I previously suggested to him that you do your primary school here in the city, but he could have none of it.'

'For real, aunty?'

'Yes. That is the truth, but anyway, we are where we are and we should be fine. You can take a nap in my bedroom if you need to rest.'

'Thank you, aunty.'

Tete's bedroom is cosy and has lots of room. Close to the door is a long shoe rake with many flat and high heeled shoes she has never seen her with in the village, as well as male ones she reckons belong Biggie. She sits on the comfy double-bed which is covered in a cream throw with decorations of red roses and lots of pillows. She slumbers onto the bed without taking off her shoes and within minutes she is fast asleep, peacefully.

Seven

Ambivalence

On a Friday morning, she wakes up late. It's now been four months since she moved to Mutare. The first few months have seen her get used to staying in the house most of the time, and to the noise. Tete has been true to her word. She had her enrolled for evening classes at a nearby community college, although Mercy is sleepy and tired all the time and bunks most of the lessons without telling her. She finds herself more in tune with the baby growing inside of her than with anything else. It kicks and rolls and scratches and causes her to want to pee all the time, and she can't wait for that day when she will be delivered of it. She dreams that it will be a little girl like her and, in a weird sense, the little sister that she wished for when she was a kid. She has now accepted that she has to move on and straighten up her life, one way or another, and that she has to truly forgive Father.

Tete is not in the house. She has already left the house at the break of dawn, as she does every day, to sell the clothing items which she sources from Mozambique at the flea market in the CBD. The clothes come in huge bales from overseas, both new and used, and, together with the other women, they buy these bales and share the contents amongst themselves. Every day, she is out of the house at dawn, and is back just in time for supper. This is normal, the way many families are surviving in the city, carried on the untiring shoulders of industrious mothers who cross the border to try and make a living.

The country has gone to the dogs.

On the other hand, Biggie, like many other men, seems to leave the house and come back at random. He doesn't have a regular job. Many nights he sleeps in the lounge on the sofa, but a few times Mercy has woken up to find that he slept in the same bed as Tete, and at other times she has woken up to strange sounds coming from Tete's bedroom in the dead of the night. She never asks about this. It is none of her business.

Today, she is in good spirits. She prepares her room and takes a long shower before collecting the few coins left on the table by Tete, so she can buy bread and eggs from the small kiosk across the road. She is about to leave her room when the door to Tete's room opens. She screams. She didn't expect anyone else to be at home.

Biggie is standing in the doorway in his boxers, no shirt, his thingy clearly marked against the shorts. He stretches and yawns, his bones making clicking sounds. Mercy stands frozen right in front of him, admiring his biceps and triceps.

'You scared me, uncle,' she says.

He smiles and yawns again, but does not cover up.

'What time is it?' he asks as he peeps into the small corridor and lounge so he can read the time displayed on the silver clock hanging against the walls, which has the shape of a teapot. 'Eleven o'clock!' he exclaims.

'Are you late?' asks Mercy, finally looking away.

'No. No work for me today. It's Friday! Oh, yeah it's Friday,' he does a little dance as he says this.

'So, are you staying at home?'

'Yes.'

'Good! It's lonely here, sometimes. Very boring. I am tired of watching cartoons on the TV day in day out.'

'Maybe I can get us a good movie from the video club?'

'Please,' she says as she slips into her flat shoes, supporting her weight against the walls in order to do this. 'Would you like to come with me to buy some bread and eggs?' she continues.

'Why not?' he says as he slips into his huge shorts and grabs a loose blue shirt. He buckles the buttons as they walk out of the yard.

They decide to take a walk to the main shops which are further up the road, walking slowly for her sake. To those who don't know them, they are like husband and wife.

On the way back to the house, after they buy their stuff from the shop whose owner has a big tummy and long beard, they sit on a concrete block of one of what used to be water drains running along the edges of the road, before the drains were filled up with sand over the years, so Mercy can have a little rest.

'This is hard work,' she says as she sits on the concrete, her right hand on her lower back.

'I can imagine,' says Biggie. 'It is a great job you women do, yet the child ends up bearing the father's name, not the mother's.'

Mercy thinks that Biggie is a gentleman for saying this. Most men consider it a privilege for a woman to carry what is obviously their child. In the village, it is not uncommon for wives to be sent packing after a fight with their husbands and to be told to 'leave my children behind.' So, Mercy did not consider it strange when Freedom once said to her that a man's depositing a child inside a woman's womb is just like someone depositing their money with a bank; the bank cannot turn around one day and claim that the money belongs to it. That is the consensus, so Biggie's saying this makes him a saint.

'So, where is the father?' he continues as they resume their walk back to the house. They stop now and again as various people, boys and girls, greet Biggie or call out his name from afar. He is quite popular.

'I don't want to talk about that,' Mercy says, without showing any emotion. 'Let's just say this child has no father, only a mother.'

'I understand. I also grew up without a father. I still don't know him, and I really don't care.'

'What about your mother?'

'She is there in the village, in Chivhu, with her current husband and children.'

'Current husband?'

'Well, I grew up seeing my mother with many different men in our house. I didn't know what to call them: *baba*, uncle or stranger. My mother always insisted that we called them father, each of the more than ten that I got to know at different points in my life, as if they were my real fathers, when in the actual fact, they were maybe father to just but one or none of the nine of us. That is why I left the stupid village.'

'So, do you go back, sometimes?'

She feels pity for him, but he doesn't seem to pity himself at all.

'No. Not at all. I have nothing to go back there for. If I die they can just bury me here, the prisoners will bury me.'

'I am sorry to hear that.'

'Why? I am okay as I am. I have survived all the fifteen years I have been here, I have always managed to fend for myself, one way or another.'

When they are back in the house, Biggie offers to cook as Mercy rests on the sofa admiring Tete's pictures which are pinned against the walls, and the polished wooden and stone souvenirs on the wood and glass display cabinet.

In a little while, Biggie brings the food in a tray and sets it on the coffee table. They sit side by side and slowly munch the food, chatting and laughing. Mercy finds Biggie to be quite funny. Now she understands why Tete fell for him.

'How old are you?' she asks, so abruptly that Biggie almost chokes from the food.

'Why?' he asks as he clears his throat and sips more tea.

'I just want to know. You are obviously much younger than aunty…'

'Love has no age. Isn't that what they say?'

'Right. But, how old are you?'

'Twenty-five.'

'For real?' Mercy is genuinely surprised. She expected him to be somewhere near or above thirty. She herself feels more than twenty. The pregnancy has made her grow up a bit. She feels more responsible.

'True. And you?'

'Well, eh, sixteen now, so a lot younger than you.'

'Only ten years younger. Tari would have been about your age when I was born. You see, I am right between the two of you, I could date you as much as I date Tari. Age is not a limiting factor.'

He laughs.

She smiles and looks away.

'Are you going to marry her?' she asks, looking back at him.

'No way. I don't think she wants that. You see, marriage sometimes spoils the love. Sometimes, one needs to enjoy life rather than complicate it.'

'I see.'

After breakfast, Mercy takes a rest on Tete's bed, pouring over a glossy colourful magazine. She marvels at the different maternity dresses she finds in it, picturing herself in each of them and feeling good.

Biggie is outside, on the grass in the front yard of the house with a bunch of other boys, boozing and puffing under the small peach tree. Mercy does not try to find out who Biggie's friends are or what they look like. She is not bothered, so she stays in the house. The boys are there until late in the afternoon, when they decide to go to the local bottle store to wind up the day before launching into a night of partying.

The film which Biggie brings from the video club turns out to be a gripping American war drama. Mercy watches the rest of it by herself as he dozes off whilst seated next to her, at one point resting his head on her lap, his head pressing against her bulging tummy. She gently strokes his shoulder and admires his peaceful sleep. She is completely lost in the film.

Tete is back to the house at night, with a number of her lady friends, a noisy bunch which laughs a lot. She is drunk, the first time Mercy sees her like this. Biggie is back on his feet and drinking again, playing loud music and turning the house into some party. Slowly, the house fills up as more of Tete's and Biggie's friends join them. Mercy enjoys the vibe, the dancing which ensues and the various Shona accents which she picks up from the revellers. She feels that she can dance way better than most of them. If it were not for the pregnancy, she would be showing them her moves right now. It brings back some memories. Memories of Chipo and Freedom and Lovemore. Memories of them running after each other at the school, dancing to the music at the village centre and swimming in the cold waters of Mupfurati. Then she remembers the humiliation which she suffered when the pregnancy was discovered, the reason why she cannot wish to be with them again. She ditches the hurtful thoughts and concentrates on the present scene.

'Drink up my niece, have some fun,' Tete urges her, speaking above the music in a loud drunken voice.

'I can't. You know I can't,' says Mercy. 'It won't be good for the baby.' She doesn't say it, but she knows that it is not acceptable for women to drink, that the ones that do are of loose morals. She doesn't want to be like them.

'Nonsense! Don't listen to everything the silly doctors tell you. If we all listened to them, we would never do anything. Drink, drink, drink.'

Tete's friends join in the chanting, urging her to drink just a little. She succumbs to the pressure, but she is not sure which bottle to use or how much to take, whether it is a good idea after all. One of the ladies pours out a Coke and Montello punch for her. She grabs it and, closing her eyes, downs it to the halfway mark. They clap their hands for her. The taste of it is as awful as it is interesting. Ambivalent. The smell of the alcohol to her is like what it used to be when Father came back from the village beerhall and insisted that Mother warmed up his food in the middle of the night Mercy would get up to help Mother and sometimes would ask her to go back to sleep so she could do it herself. She felt pity for her, but she understood that it was good for a wife to do her husband's bidding, even if the man was a lapping dog.

She grabs the glass again and slowly sips the drink until it is finished. Then she pours another. And another. By midnight she is dancing like an unpregnant thirteen-year-old, very much intoxicated.

She doesn't remember much of last night when she wakes up. She finds herself in Biggie's arms, in Tete's bedroom, Biggie soundly asleep between Tete and her, Tete's arms wrapped around his waist from behind and his rested on her tummy in turn. Like three puppies in a sleeping basket. Biggie is shirtless although she and Tete are fully dressed apart from having no shoes on their feet. She slowly unbuckles his hands, lifts up his left arm and eases herself, or rather falls, out of the bed. It is not easy. She has to sit on the floor first and turn around like an elephant, supporting her weight against the headboard in order to get up to her feet. Her head hurts badly, like it has been split right through the middle with a sharp axe. The baby inside her kicks and spins and makes her weak. She drags herself into the kitchen and drinks some water.

Eight

Tribulation

When the time comes, it is in the night and she is alone in the house Tete is in Mozambique and Biggie is out with the boys. At first it is like a passing wave, then, in a short space of time, the waves are coming and coming, stronger and stampeding over each other, the pain waxing more and more until she has difficulty moving from her bedroom. She groans and screams and mumbles but no-one comes through the door. Her screams are really not going much further than the thick brick walls. She tries crawling to the door, but she can barely move her legs due to the reverting pain. She drags herself on her butt, in a sitting position, along the cold cement floor in the corridor until she is in the middle of the lounge-cum-kitchen-cum-dining room. She lies on the floor and writhes in pain, resisting the urge both to throw her legs wide open or to cross them. She feels as if the baby would just jettison out if she opens them any further and as if she would squash its head if she closes them.

She has almost lost hope when the key turns in the hole and Biggie walks in, jollily unaware of what he is walking into. 'Mercy!' he screams as he runs towards her and kneels by her side. 'Is everything okay?'

'Call the ambulance,' she says.

'Is the baby coming?'

'Just call the bloody ambulance!'

Biggie fumbles for his phone in his pocket. He holds it in his trembling hands and tries dialling before it slips to the ground and flips open, the battery falling out. He picks it up and puts the battery back in, then closes the back cover. Meanwhile, Mercy is groaning and grumbling and murmuring.

'What number do I call?' asks Biggie.

'The ambulance!'

'I don't know the number. What do I do now?'

He truly doesn't know what to do.

He grabs the phone directory from Tete's bedroom but he is not literate enough to know where to look. He turns the pages randomly before he decides to go out of the house and knock at the neighbours'.

When he comes back he has on his tail the elderly couple that lives next door, Mbuya Pongozi and her husband. The husband is on the phone as Mbuya Pongozi and Biggie attend to Mercy. They lift her onto Tete's bed.

'Is he coming?' asks Mbuya Pongozi, to her husband.

'Yes,' the old man replies, stepping back outside through the main door in the back of the house.

He waits on the street for his son who lives just a few streets away, and within minutes he arrives in a small Datsun sedan which has only two doors and a noisy engine. They bundle Mercy into the back seat through the folded passenger seat. Mbuya Pongozi sits with her in the back, Biggie in the front.

Soon, they are at the hospital and being rushed to the maternity ward by hospital staff. Biggie thanks the driver, profusely, and runs alongside the wheelchair, along the corridor with flickering lights, together with the nurses.

'Sir, are you the husband?' asks one of the nurses along the way.

'Yes. No,' he says in a confused manner.

'Which is which now?'

'She is my sister.'

'Okay. So, you wait here,' she says when they get to the double doors. 'We will let you know when she is delivered.'

They wheel her into the inner room and leave Biggie in the small waiting area.

There is nobody else there, until Mbuya Pongozi joins him minutes later and sits next to him. She could not rush like them.

He is unsettled. He has never been in such a situation before.

'She will be fine,' reassures Mbuya Pongozi, who can see the worry in his eyes.

'I hope so.'

'How long was she like that?'

'I had just come in when I found her screaming, lying on the floor. I was not in the house.'

'Don't worry, you will be a father soon.'

Biggie does not respond. It is obvious that the neighbours do not have an idea who he is to Tete. Or is it that they simply refuse to accept that he is old enough to be her boyfriend? He knows he should feel offended. He looks at her wrinkled face and forgives her. It's not her fault, he thinks. That is what society has shaped her to believe, and besides, what does an old woman who has had all her juices sucked out by life know about love?

'I went through all this. Eight times,' she continues. 'Now all my children are out of school. But they refuse to marry. You are lucky to have such a pretty wife, so don't worry my child. Once she delivers she won't remember the pain, not even a bit.'

'I hope so.'

He takes out his packet of Madison and is about to light one when he comes face to face with the sign that reads

NO SMOKING, in red, with a crossed-out picture of a cigarette. He understands, he has seen the picture before. He puts the cigarette back into its packet and walks towards the exit, leaving the old woman sitting alone on the bench in the corridor.

It is now more than five hours since they have been in the hospital and now in the early hours of morning. Biggie and Mbuya Pongozi are still waiting in the corridor. He is nervous and worried as if he is the father of the child. Not for himself, but for Mercy, for what she must be going through and for the safety of the child. Until now, he didn't notice the affection now grown between them. He reflects on his answer to the nurse when she asked him who he was The answer was not too far away from the truth. She is now like that to him, a little sister. He feels a sense of responsibility towards her, perhaps in the way that he should be feeling towards his own siblings. The one thing that he still doesn't understand, however, perhaps for fear of exploring what he knows would be dangerous, is why people just assume that he is responsible for Mercy's pregnancy, that he is her husband. Many times he's had to explain that he is just an uncle and not a boyfriend, that it is her aunt that he's hooked up with. The explanation has mostly been met with surprise, or laughter, or both. He is fed up of it.

'Why are they taking so long?' Mbuya Pongozi interrupts his thoughts. 'Is something gone wrong?'

She has simply echoed what is in Biggie's mind.

'I will ask them,' he says, then walks to the door and knocks.

An assistant opens one of the double doors. 'Any problem?' she asks, looking at Biggie from top to bottom as if measuring him.

'How is she doing?'

'We will let you know when it's done.'

'What's happening? I need to know why this is taking so long.'

'This is labour, mister, it's not like eating *sadza*. That's why you men should just stay away from this business.'

'But, is everything okay?'

'Did you not hear what I just said?' she says with an attitude. 'We will let you know.'

Annoyed, Biggie walks away.

The assistant shakes her head and watches him walk along the corridor with the few flickering lights and many dead ones, then she closes the door.

He gets to the end of the corridor and out into the open. It is deserted outside and poorly lit, except for the distant sporadic lights of the CBD. He leans against the building and lights up a cigarette using matches. He draws in hard and long and holds the smoke in his closed mouth for a long time, allowing some of it to puff through his nostrils as if through a chimney, then he blows out slowly through his mouth like he is whistling, savouring the moment and getting lost inside his own head. He reminisces about his time in the village and, for once in a long time, wonders about his mother and siblings, where they could be and what they could be doing at this hour. He wonders about his father, who he could be and whether his mother would tell him if he were to press her hard. The thought of a father that he never had makes him sick. How could someone just impregnate a woman and leave them to fend for themselves like that, leaving the child to suffer the consequences of his own stupidity as if he were some cow? It is not as if children apply to come into the world anyway, but a consequence of two people selfishly poking into each other and both or one of them reaching a climax. And, who in their right mind gives a child a name such as Bigman, as his full name is called? Maybe his father was a big man, like Dhorofiya perhaps, who is famed for carrying his oversized wife on his shoulders whilst running away from the guerrillas during the liberation war because he was afraid they could snatch her away from him for being a traitor. It is because of this reason, the futility of life, that Biggie decided a long time ago that he would never marry, that he would never have children. The same reason why he spends so much energy in the makeshift gym at his friend's, Trymore's, backyard, and why he doesn't have the luxury of experiencing emotion. Why bother having children who would live to regret the day that they were born?

As these thoughts run up and down his head one more time, he can't help but realise that Mercy is about to create a replica of him, a child with a father who is not there and will never be there. He curses the ground and stumps the cigarette against the white wall before hurriedly walking back inside as if someone is calling after his name.

What bothers Mercy is not the fact that they did not immediately bring the baby to her, but that she did not hear it cry. She didn't have the chance to look at and cuddle her baby like she saw on TV. The baby was whisked away from her as soon as she felt the release. She is tired. In the end they had to pull the baby out using this thing that sucked and pulled out his head as she could not push anymore.

'Where is my baby?' she asks one of the midwives in the room, in a tired voice.

'Don't worry, they will bring him soon.'

'It's a boy?'

She sounds happy and seems to have forgotten that she wished for a girl. She will now have to put away all the pinks and yellows that she stocked up at the house. All she wants now is to see her baby.

'Yes,' replies the midwife.

'Why did he not cry?'

'I don't know. It happens sometimes.'

'I want my baby now. Please. I want to see my baby.'

She will not be convinced until she sees him. She thinks that she might have had a still birth. 'Please tell me my baby is fine,' she continues.

'He is fine. They are just doing some checks on him.'

The few minutes are like hours to her and she can no longer be calm. Now she is sitting on the bed and her stomach churning. All sorts of ideas go through her head. Her attempted abortion completely forgotten, all she cares for now is to see her son.

Finally, the doctor opens the door, a smile on his face.

'Is my son okay?'

'Yes, my dear. He is fine.'

Although he tries to keep calm, Mercy can sense the apprehension in his voice. Something is not right, she thinks.

'Is that all?'

'No. There is something that you need to know.'

'What?'

The doctor smiles again and says, 'Your son is in good health, but he has some physical challenges...'

He pauses and looks at Mercy, whose mouth is open, then continues, 'He has a condition. Some of his limbs were not developed to maturity, so you will notice that one leg is not quite there, and his spinal cord is not as straight. He might have difficulty sitting or walking without assistance.'

'But why? Why?' Mercy screams. 'Why does it have to be me all the time? Why me?' She cries and appeals to a higher power that she is increasingly doubtful exists, to the god of Mother who did not come to her rescue when Father raped her, the god who has failed her again.

'Madam, I know this is difficult, but you have to accept that children are a gift from God. We do not determine what they will be like, we are just given them the way they are. You see, disability does not mean inability, it is just a form that is different from that of the majority.'

'Can I see him?'

'Oh yes, you can.'

He calls for the boy and two of the midwives bring him, wrapped up in a blue hospital towel. He is crying in a faint voice and is pale in complexion. She holds him in her arms and loves him. He looks like Father - the nose, the mouth and the shape of the head. She hesitates to unwrap the towel to reveal the legs. She carefully rests him on her lap to undo the wrap, then she breaks down again.

'Tribulation,' she says.

'What?' the doctor asks.

'That is his name. Tribulation.'

The doctor and the midwives look at each other but make no comment.

'Would you like to keep him, given his condition?' asks the doctor.

'Of course. He is my child, I carried him for nine months.'

'That's good, but if you ever change your mind, the hospital has a scheme. We can adopt him.'

'No. I will look after my child,' she says, kissing the forehead of Tribulation.

Nine

The *kombi* ride

Father does not come to see the baby who looks like him. Mother doesn't either. Both dread the idea of it, the fact that the child is said to be a replica of Father. Mercy doesn't care and has no plans at all of visiting the village.

After a few days in the hospital she is ready to go home, to Tete's rented house in the city. Biggie shows up to take her home, with a whole *kombi* omnibus of which he is the conductor, the *hwindi*, full of passengers ruefully diverted from their normal route. The passengers are complaining about the opportunities and quality time with their families and friends which they will miss as a result, but Biggie and his driver friend, Mundewere, do not really care. They simply ignore them as they pull up at the hospital's main entrance where Mercy is sitting outside on a bag full of clothes, holding the little man who is wrapped up in swaddling clothes of blue and brown and white. She smiles and gets up to her feet when she sees Biggie who rushes to grab the bag so he can tie it to the outside railings of the vehicle, on the outside carrier.

'So, you bring us all this way just to pick up your wife?' one of the passengers, a middle-aged man, complains, popping his head through the window to hurl insults at Biggie. 'Why not hire a taxi, hey you *hwindi*, why not hire a taxi? You think we are your wives, huh?'

'She must be loved that wife of yours,' says another, a young man with an uneven box haircut. 'She looks pretty though, like she's not had a baby at all. So, people, please relax. The lady deserves it. I would do the same for my queen, certainly. Damn man! Your woman is very fine …'

The other passengers laugh at the exchange, which is really not an exchange as both Biggie and the driver completely ignore the scolding.

Mercy sits quietly in the front, next to the driver, on a seat reserved for her, with no seat belt around her and with Tribulation on her lap. She holds him in her arms like she is holding a crate full of eggs, feeling important and certainly not oblivious to Biggie's kindness in doing this for her. She is impressed, but she says nothing as the *kombi* jerks forwards with the door still open. Biggie runs alongside it and for a while perilously hangs by the open sliding door as the vehicle skids away. He squeezes himself inside as it turns the corner, and he is thrust onto the lap of an elderly woman who slaps his butt with her bare hands.

Mercy balances and stabilises herself, stretching her hand to hold the dashboard so that she and Tribulation are not thrown right through the windscreen. She looks down at Tribulation to adore him, and occasionally raises up her head to look at Biggie and smile, and at the road and houses sprinting in the opposite direction. It is a rough ride, typical of the *kombis*, with the vehicle veering and swerving and cutting corners, but she does not feel much of it as her mind is preoccupied with her Tribulation. She does not have a chance to think much about anything else these days, but him; how lovely he looks, how she will provide for him and how happy she is to hold in her arms the thing that wriggled and caused havoc inside her belly for so many months. He dominates her world. If she is not feeding him, she is bathing him or getting him to sleep or to stop crying. She loves him so much that she does not have time to worry anymore about how this handsome boy got deposited inside of her in the first place, how she wrestled under the weight of Father and bit him on the arm before he stuffed her yellow dress into her open mouth to contain her screaming and pinned her arms against the squeaky bed, how he heaved and sweated on top of her as he forced himself between her legs, how she gave up the fight and wished she was dead. These thoughts which bothered her before, of the pain that she felt when he tore into her flesh and broke that little thing inside her depth, of the emotional anger and pain and stress that she felt afterwards, of the lies and the tying of the tummy and the shame, all these, have not at all crossed her mind since she held him in her arms. All she cares for now is him and how she will go back to school and sit her exams and provide for him.

They drop her off at the house, amidst more agitated protests and insults from the angry passengers, before they proceed on their planned journey to Zimunya. Biggie and Mundewere are still unmoved by the insults. They are used to receiving these daily from the passengers and other *kombi* operators, and to dishing out the same, not sparingly, to other passengers and ordinary people on the street for no particular reason. Instead, they laugh, Biggie reassuring the passengers that whatever they hope to find at home will still be waiting for them when they get there. '*Musatombotya vabereki, bhora pasi ndege mudenga*,' he says.

Mercy inside the house, after Biggie helped her as the *kombi* waited by the gate, finds that Tete is not there as she is in Mozambique. She is pleased to find her single mattress replaced with a new one, and on the bedside a brand-new Moses-basket with a comfy interior. The room looks cleaner too, and has been repainted. She admires the clean walls, thinking to herself that this could only have been done by Biggie. She pictures him in dirty overalls and boots, wielding a brush dripping with the cream paint, whistling as he goes up and down the walls for her. She smiles back at this picture inside her head, telling herself that she is lucky to have such an uncle. She observed him when he opened the door for her moments ago, how he reached over her shoulder from behind to see the face of Tribulation and commented about how handsome and lovely he is. But privately, unknown to her, Biggie was thinking, and still thinks, that it is unfair for Mercy to have been given this burden by whoever hands out burdens to people, of bringing up such a challenged child alone. If it were up to him, he would have given up the child to the hospital.

When Tete arrives back from Mozambique, Biggie is not at home. The taxi driver who drops her off, the same one who brought them home the day Mercy came from the village, carries the huge bag of blue and purple stripes, full of second hand clothes which include jeans and t-shirts, shirts and dresses and bras which many lucky children from the suburbs will be glad to have for Christmas, it being the only time that they are really guaranteed, almost, of having new clothes, almost, upon which they will dump their old garments for the new and wait for next Christmas. Business is brisk for the hawkers in this festive season.

Tete sings and dances, and ululates and shrills, with happiness. She is not drunk, she sings for her nephew who has now come home, who she reckons is like a son to her. There has never been a baby in the house since she started living here five years ago.

Mercy is happy to see Tete again after what felt like ages since she came to the hospital singing and drawing the attention of the entire hospital wing, before she left to go to the village to tell Father and Mother of the good news. After which she left again for Mozambique. She is a hardworking woman. One whose footsteps Mercy should emulate and follow. When she is fully recovered and her son weaned from the milk, she will travel with her to Mozambique. She will open her own market stall and look after her child.

'The man is in the house,' Tete says as she throws her handbag across the room, onto the empty seat, and plunges into the sofa next to Mercy. She takes the baby, who was sleeping when she arrived but has since woken up because of the noise, and is now busy crying, away from her.

'Stop crying sweetie, oh sweetie, did I wake you up sweetie? Stop crying my man,' she says as she rocks him up in her arms and pushes back the blanket to see his face clearly.

He stops crying as if he understood what she just said, then he desperately starts fumbling for milk with his mouth against Tete's blouse.

'You, cheeky little boy,' she says. 'I don't have any milk for you. And you keep changing appearances, huh, first you looked like my brother, and now like Sekuru Chigodho …'

She hands him back to Mercy after he resumes crying, as the taxi-man who entered the house at the same time as Tete waves goodbye. 'Later, madam,' he says as he makes his way through the door, Tete paying him very little attention. 'Thanks,' she says without looking, as she slips her feet out of her soiled tennis shoes.

'How are you, aunty?' Mercy asks when she is assured of her attention. 'Did you travel well?'

'Yes, I did. Has he been a good boy, Tribe?'

'Yes. He's not been as bad as I expected.'

'Good,' says Tete as she takes to her feet, picks up her purse and starts for her bedroom. 'I am tired,' she says with a yawn. 'Where is Biggie? Did he look after you at all since you came back or has he just been busy boozing?'

'Ah, Tete, he is a man. How much did you expect from him? He did his best.'

'Good.'

Tete disappears into her bedroom and in a few minutes, she is fast asleep, in her day clothes. The journey from Beira is long and the transport overcrowded. Hoarding from there as opposed to nearby Manica is what allows her to get a bit more out of her trade. And she isn't doing badly at all, for a woman that is. At least she is able to pay the rent and buy food and entertainment, especially as Biggie really brings nothing home. After all, his job as a *hwindi* does not have a guaranteed income as the owners of the different vehicles he spends the day marshalling have no knowledge at all of his involvement in their affairs, or of his existence even. All he does is help his driver friends and hope that they give him a bit of cash at the end of the day, enough for him to come back tomorrow for another handout. Every day, he wakes up in the morning to go to the terminus in the CBD with no idea at all what he will do for the day or how much he will earn from it, except that he is guaranteed free transport to wherever he wants to go since he is known by all drivers and other *hwindis* in the town. He always finds a place to squeeze into a *kombi,* even when it is full, fuller than the legal specifications of the manufacturers and government regulations. Dangerously full. He would just make it inside the vehicle before closing its door, bending his torso forward for as long as it takes and hanging in that painful position for which he no longer feels the pain. It is normal. This is life for him and he is happy.

Thus, Tete is really the breadwinner of the house as she has to provide for him and herself, and now for Mercy and Tribulation. She doesn't mind. It makes her indispensable and gives her the latitude to do whatever she wants in the house.

When Biggie gets home, Tete and Mercy have already gone to bed, Mercy only for a few minutes as Tribulation kept her awake because of his incessant crying. She later figured out that his crying was due to stomach pains and so she administered to him a bit of cooking oil which she boiled on the two-plate stove.

Biggie bangs the door as if he were some policeman and, having been half asleep anyway, Mercy gets up to open it for him.

It is around 1:30am.

When he steps inside the house he is cursing.

'It happened again,' he says. 'S**t! It's a mess ...' He shakes his head furiously, like a goat shaking off rain water.

Mercy stands there without saying a word, following him with her eyes as he stumbles to the sofa to sit.

He is not drunk.

She shuts the door and locks it. 'What happened to your keys?' she asks.

'Keys, keys, keys. They were in the dash, yes, in the dashboard. S**t!'

'What's the matter uncle?'

'It's a mess. A real mess. Is Tari back?'

'Yes, she is. She came back this afternoon.'

'Good!'

'Can I warm up the food for you?' she asks. She doesn't understand why Biggie is so on edge like this. She has never before seen him this way. She is concerned.

'No, don't bother. It's the bloody accident. They all died, all of them in the little car, and Mundewere. Mundewere is dead.'

'Who is Mundewere?'

'The driver of course. It was a head on. Bang! The lights were not working properly, the dip. I kept telling him. Fix these things, the dip. It was not working. But he didn't listen, Mundewere.'

'I am sorry uncle.'

'All the people in the car died. And Mundewere. Now the police want to question me again. What do I say? The *kombi* was too full and there is a lot of injured persons. They are all pointing at me, a *hwindi*. But what do I know about this? I was not driving. I am just a plain ordinary *hwindi*.'

Mercy feels pity for him, but she can't do anything. She feels that she owes him a good deed. Having nothing else to offer, she stretches out her arms for a hug. Him half-rising from the sofa and pressing against her breasts, which are slightly visible through the thin pyjamas and which smell of baby milk, they embrace for a moment. As he wraps his arms around her waist, his mind is drawn again to how beautifully built she is, how the baby has not inflicted any serious damage to her figure. If anything, it seems to have made her even more beautiful. He pauses like that, in the embrace, before Tete's coughing interrupts them. She is standing just behind them with a long towel covering the upper and middle part of her body, her smooth legs and toughened knees exposed.

'Hi babe,' Biggie says to Tete as they unbuckle, smiling. The embrace lasted only for a moment, but enough to send his brain on a sprint.

'Now I see what you two have been up to in my absence,' Tete says. Smiling.

Mercy feels awkward. Although she and Biggie have never thought of each other that way, she in the moment just gone felt an unsettling attraction beyond the pity that she felt for him. She smiles, shyly, before Tribulation comes to the rescue. He cries his heart out as if something bad has happened to him. She gladly walks away from the scene to her room, hurriedly.

'Welcome back, sweetie,' Biggie says confidently, and moves to kiss Tete on the cheek. 'Did you bring anything nice for me?'

'Me of course. What more did you want?' Tete says as she walks to the fridge and grabs a bottle of Mazoe orange drink She pours it into a blue plastic cup. Biggie follows her and grabs her from behind.

'Get away, you,' she says, 'and stop pretending that you missed me when you were busy hitting it with the young girls when I was away.'

'I did miss you, darling. Truly,' he says as he nibbles her right ear, teasingly.

'Stop it, Biggie,' she whispers, 'we have a child in the house. Well, children.' She turns around and gently shoves him away with an elbow.

He sits on the single seat as she drinks the juice in one go, wondering how he is going to tell her about the accident. The last time that he was arrested, which was the third time that she bailed him out and for which he actually was innocent, she warned him to put his house in order, or else she would be forced to look for other alternatives to their arrangement. This shook him badly afterwards, when he thought about it, when it hit him hard that he has nothing of his own which he could turn to if that happened, that he would pretty much be destitute or end up squatting with his friends one night at a time. It occurred to him that he was terribly lucky to have Tete in his life. In that moment, he even considered whether he should marry her, without paying the *lobola* of course as he had nothing with which to do that, if she agreed. It turned out that it was only wonderful day dreaming. It would be too obvious to her what he wanted, so he resorted to satisfying her in other ways as much as he could, giving himself like no other man can and making himself indispensable that way. That plan seems to be working just fine as Tete responds more to him than the other girls that he occasionally cheats her with, boosting his performance by eating herbs sold in the Sakubva market by some woman who hails from Gokwe.

'Mundewere is dead,' he says, bluntly.

Tete drops the Mazoe plastic bottle that she was about to return into the fridge. 'Mundewere? You mean Mundewere, the driver?' she asks.

'Yes, he died in the accident.'

'The accident ...'

'Yes. I was with him.'

He pauses as Tete is picking up the bottle, putting it back onto the table and sitting onto the arm of the seat next to him. He waits for the response, for the flurry of hurtful words that he knows will be coming, but they don't.

'The police want to talk to me,' he continues.

Then the words rain on him, rapidly and with great fury: 'There you go again, Biggie. The police, again! When really is this going to stop? Is this a thug-house that you have the police knocking on my door now and again? My door. My house. Last time you said never again, that you would look for a job, but here you are. Again. What kind of a man are you who relies on a woman for everything? Is it only sex that you are good at? This running around with the *kombis* for peanuts, what good is it really? You need to grow up, get a licence and start driving. Get an income. Yes. Be a man and not a boy. Tomorrow, oh yes tomorrow, you need to register at the community centre for evening classes to cure that ignorance of yours. You are too young to not be able to read and write. You need to get that licence, whatever you do, whether you bribe or what I don't care. I just need to see that licence in this house. That is the only way we can stop this rubbish…'

'I can read. I can write …,' Biggie protests.

'Then get the bloody provisional licence!'

'Sweetie, I am sorry.'

'I am tired of this your sorry, so please drop it.'

He doesn't argue any further. He takes off his shoes and follows Tete to bed. They sleep facing the walls, in opposite directions, inwardly regretting the whole situation. Later, in the middle of the night, after spending hours like that and both failing to get sleep despite each pretending to be, they pretend to forget their quarrel and silently turn to face each other. Their business finished, they go back to sleep silently, and in no time at all they are both sleeping like babies, facing opposite directions. Tete is too tired to dream of anything. Biggie is not. He dreams that he is back in the village and in school, with Mercy. They are laughing and running after each other. He is extremely happy. Then, one of his mother's men tries to take Mercy away from him. He fights him with an iron bar until he flies away in a whirlwind. Then they kiss, he and Mercy. At this point he smiles, in the dream and in his sleep, that if the lights were on and Tete awake, she would notice the dimples that form on his cheeks.

Ten

The circle

The next time Tete finds Biggie and Mercy too close and personal, she doesn't take it lightly. When they go to bed that night she tells him, with words big and small, to stay away from her niece Nothing changes, however, for when she comes back from the market, as she now does often and impromptu, she always finds the two happily together. It troubles her and slowly nibbles at her heart for a whole six months, until Tribulation is almost a year old.

Father and Mother still haven't been to see Tribulation although they always send their regards with Tete when she visits them in the village. They don't ask much about him either and they seem to be bothered by his disability. They would rather not come too close and have the guilt further ingrained into their conscience. They will stay away until forced by circumstances. It still bothers Mother that Ruby failed to stop all this from happening despite her mother having done a fantastic job for her many years ago. At that time, when she sought after Ruby's mother's services, on her own, the procedure was flawless. It allowed her to have her youth back, to manage society's dubious standards until she was ready to get married. It didn't work out with Ruby, and her failure did not only see Mother lose her RW position, but also relegated her to the laughing stock of the village, losing even Mapudege's respect. Clearly, Ruby's mother did not teach her well.

Chipo, Tete says, is retaking some of her subjects at the village school after she failed to garner the required 5 O Levels. Freedom has re-joined his father in Harare, and Lovemore, well, he couldn't even take the exams. Father, of course, continues to be Mai Mercy's husband.

A cholera outbreak has claimed the lives of many villagers, Chief Kamutsi being one of those recently promoted into the realm of the ancestors. He has been gone for a few months now, and has been replaced by his eldest son, Chisindi. Chief Chisindi, as he is now called, has already made lots of controversial decisions, so much that the villagers loathe him just as much as they adored his father. Every weekend, Tete says, there is a meeting of the village elders at his compound, new laws are pronounced, huge beasts slaughtered, and lagers opened.

Thursday is now Chief's Day, whence no-one is allowed in the fields, and Tuesdays, they all take turns, household by household, to fetch water for Chief Chisindi's compound. No-one dares disobey his commandments as the punishment could be severe, ranging from a fine of several herds of livestock to total banishment from the village. The people are not happy, but what can they do? They pin their hopes on Mangwiro, for he is now an elder in the Chief's Council and seems to be the only one with a whole brain.

It is because of a lack of options that Tete leaves Mercy and Biggie alone in the house when she visits the village for three nights.

Mercy has no clue about her suspicion. She is busy not only enjoying Biggie's attention, but now thinks of their friendship as something that was meant to be. She even feels jealous when he and Tete snugly sit together on the sofa and kiss each other on the lips. With Tribulation now able to play on his own, lying on his back that is, Mercy can now move around and bask in the sunshine in the morning against the outside walls of the house, and now takes time to talk with the other girls, running up and down the streets like a normal teenager. The pregnancy now a piece of history, the clothes which she chooses from Tete's stocks suit her very well. She tries to keep up with the trends on the streets of Mutare. She is shy at first, to put on the mini-skirts, but with time and seeing Tete donning such every time she goes out, these become like second nature to her. This delights Biggie, who observes this from the corner of his eye when Tete is present, and who now spends a lot more time at home despite Tete's complaining about his lack of a job.

With Tete in the village, Mercy and Biggie are free to run after each other and to play all sorts of hide-and-seek in the house. The growing attraction between them is quite obvious, but that is where it should end. Mercy is keenly aware of Biggie's being a no-go area, although she does fantasise about him.

The first night Tete is away, they watch movies until the early hours of the morning. Then they fall asleep next to each other, on the sofa, and are only awakened when Tribulation cries for his milk. It is then that Mercy retires to her bedroom, after feeding him cow milk which she grabs from the fridge since he has been weaned from her milk.

The second night he almost kisses her, when they are sitting on the sofa, before she snaps back into her senses. 'No,' she says as she pulls back, her heart running wild. 'Uncle! You were about to kiss me.'

'Well, does it matter, really?' Biggie says. 'Isn't the elders say you are as good as my wife? You are my *muramu*, so of course, I was going to kiss you.'

'No uncle. Aunty would kill you. And me.'

'Of course she would. Am I not worth dying for?'

'You are crazy,' she says as she gets up to her feet and retires to her bedroom.

When she is lying on her bed, she feels bad for not having allowed him to kiss her a little, because she did want him to, and for feeling that way. Kissing on its own would have been harmless for, after all, it is true that she is his *muramu*.

The tension between them growing, the time moves ever so slowly. Mercy can't wait for Tete to return, to cool down the temperatures. She doesn't trust herself anymore. She doesn't understand the feelings brewing up inside of her.

'Mercy,' Biggie says when he finds her cooking on the paraffin stove after a power blackout hits the town. The room is dimly lit with a candle placed on the window seal and another in Mercy's bedroom. Tribulation is lying on a small mattress by the side of the sofa, giggling and kicking out his little legs.

'Yes uncle,' she says as she turns away from the pot of *sadza* she's been stirring on the stove, to look at him.

'Why do you hate me?'

'Hate you, uncle?'

'Yes. I thought I was your friend. That you cared for me?'

'Of course I do.'

'Really?' he says with a smile. 'Let me tell you what I think. I think that you find me attractive, and you hate me for that.'

'What makes you say so, uncle?' she says, turning back to her cooking pot.

Biggie moves closer to her in the dimness. She feels his movement and his presence without even looking, like he is a huge magnet and she a metal nail. She closes her eyes and cringes when he rubs her bare shoulders from behind. 'You are very beautiful,' he whispers. She freezes and stops mixing the *sadza*, a rush of blood rising up to her face, her brain sending the wrong signals to the right places. She feels her body tighten, then weaken, as he moves even closer and wraps his arms around her waist from behind, tormenting her.

'Uncle,' she says, weakly. 'Stop it.'

Holding her in his huge arms, he nibbles at her ear, gently, and she feels her defences giving in. She turns around to face him, leaving the *sadza* seething by itself on the stove. In a matter of minutes, they are wrestling on the floor, him on top, she under him and Tribulation crying next to them. No-one pays attention to his cries until the referee blows the whistle, after which Mercy silently grabs her son and locks herself up in her room, in tears, leaving Biggie to finish off the cooking on his own.

A sense of guilt weighs down on her. She refuses to eat despite Biggie's insistence. He doesn't stay in the house either; he leaves for the beerhall.

Mercy feels stupid. Cheap. Violated.

'What just happened?' she asks herself as she rolls Tribulation out of her arms onto the mattress. Although she saw it coming, she didn't think she would have the guts to go through with it. She wanted to stop him when he pinned her down to the floor, but she didn't. She regrets having fallen into his trap. All she wanted was to prove to herself that she is still attractive, that she is still capable of landing a handsome guy just like him. But what was supposed to be a pleasurable moment turned out to be a nightmare. What more with the images of Father on top of her flashing across her mind like a movie in replay. Biggie was very much on top of her like Father was back then. It felt like she was being raped all over again. It ignited the very same emotions of that fateful day two years ago. No pleasure. Just pain. She feels it now just like she felt it then. There is no difference. Now she hates Biggie. And Father.

She cries her heart out the entire night. She is right back in the circle. The circle of pain.

When Tete comes back to the house in the afternoon, Biggie is still away.

Mercy is sitting outside, with Tribulation. She does not rise up to welcome Tete who is carrying a sack full of village goodies balanced on her head, a colourful shawl wrapped around her waist, and black tennis shoes on her feet. She is normally dressed like this when she visits the village, like the decent women from there, not like the useless city women.

'Welcome aunty,' Mercy says.

She remains seated, subdued.

'Are you alright, niece?' Tete asks, putting down the sack by the gate, noticing the lack of excitement in her niece.

'Yes. I am fine. I just have a little headache.'

'Oh no. Since when? Did you take any Cafemol?'

'Yes, I did.'

'Is Biggie in the house?'

'No.'

Just then, as they are still talking, Biggie arrives aboard an old Peugeot pick-up truck driven by one of his friends, Canaan. He jumps out and slams the door as Canaan releases the brakes and shoots away, leaving behind a familiar stench inspired by petrol.

He walks to Tete and kisses her on the lips. 'I missed you, babe,' he says.

'For real?' Tete asks. Then she smiles.

'Of course, babe. Who else in this world gets me like you do?'

Mercy looks at him. Then at Tete. She feels pity for her, for her lack of knowledge, and for herself, for her ungratefulness to the only woman who truly loved her when all she deserved was shame. Her mind is back in the village, in Ruby's hut. She can see Mother, her face and Ruby's looking at her imposingly, their eyes pressing her to drink the stinking liquid which was meant to terminate her Tribulation. She pictures him, her son, holding him in her arms for the first time and the doctor smiling down at her. She feels nauseated. Her head is merrily spinning around.

She looks at Biggie and hates him. She gets up to her feet and, in a huff, hurries off into the house with her son, leaving Tete and Biggie standing outside.

'Is she alright?' Tete asks.

'I don't know. Did you travel well?'

'Yes, I did. But those buses, hey, very painful. Did you look after your niece or did you just let her do all the chores by herself, you being the king as usual?'

'Oh Tari, what do you take me for? A monster or what? You remember when you used to go to Beira, when Tribulation was still very little, did I not look after them both? Now you ask me if I looked after them? Of course, I did. After all she is my *muramu*, a little you.'

'*Muramu*, right. I hope you know where to draw the line,' Tete says, not smiling.

'Let's go into the house, jealousy woman,' Biggie says.

He lifts up the sack.

Tete smiles. She follows him into the house.

It is a wonderful night. Mercy has composed herself a little, and forgotten about her pretended illness. She chats away with Tete, about the village, and Chief Chisindi, and Mother. And never about what happened between her and Biggie when she was away. Tete tells her how Mother and Father and Chipo long to see her, how they long for her to visit the village so they can see Tribulation.

Mercy assures her that she will not be visiting the village anytime soon. 'I want go back to school,' she says.

'That's my girl. In January you should start. We can make a plan for Tribulation. You are very clever, niece, we can't afford to waste your brains. You should write those exams, even in June you can do it.'

'Not with Tribulation, aunty. I will take them in November.'

'That's the attitude,' agrees Biggie. He looks at Mercy and searches her eyes to discern her reaction. She doesn't look at him at all, but looks away at the TV.

'I will go to bed now,' she says.

'Me too,' says Tete. 'I am very tired. I will stay at home this week, then I will be heading to Chimoio. Will you come with me sweetheart? We have to replenish our stocks big time.'

She now gets her stuff from the town of Chimoio. That way she can go early in the morning and come back before midnight.

'Why not, babe?' Biggie agrees. 'As long as Mercy will be okay here, alone with Tribulation.'

'I will be fine.'

Mercy and Biggie's iniquity remains covered and hidden. Apart from them avoiding eye contact, everything is back to normal, just as it was before Tete's visit to the village. But it doesn't stop Mercy from worrying about her missed period. It has now been a week and she doesn't know what to do, whether she should tell Biggie. She can't stomach it, the idea of falling pregnant again by someone who is her relative, someone who should be like a father to her. Again.

She is happy when, after almost a week, she wakes up to realise that she is not pregnant after all. Extremely relieved. She will never make such a mistake again, she vows. She visits the local pharmacy and gets herself family-planning tablets. She does question herself though, why she needs them, whether this is not preparing one's self for failure, for a repeat of something that should never happen again. Nevertheless, she does get them, and keeps them hidden in her new green oversize purse which is big enough to take in a few baby clothes and nappies.

Meanwhile, Biggie continues to behave as if nothing at all happened between them.

She uses the pills religiously, following the guidelines illustrated on the packet. Then it happens again, just when she thinks that she is winning. This time she has no one to blame but her own carnality. She doesn't know why she comes out of the shower in the morning with only a towel wrapped around her body, when Biggie is still in bed and Tete has already left for the flea market. She enters Tete's room, unwraps the towel and sits by the old dressing table, very much aware of Biggie's presence in the room. Playing with the fire. A deer walking into Cecil the lion's den.

She is sitting there, carefully and generously applying the lotion to her naked body, admiring herself in the mirror.

When Biggie wakes up, the gates of heaven are wide open before his eyes. He doesn't say a word. He has already devoured every aspect of her nakedness when she finally notices. Quickly, shyly, she wraps the towel around her body, twice dropping it to the floor in the process, but she doesn't leave the room.

'Look away,' she says.

He does. Then he offers to help rub the lotion onto her back, where her hands cannot reach. She agrees and slowly, surely, it happens. Again.

It happens again two weeks later, and four and five and six weeks later, during Tribulation's birthday party held at the house, and today, in the early hours of this Monday morning. It happens again.

She very much knows that she should not be doing this, but she feels powerless, like she has climbed into a muddy hole that's too deep for her to climb out of. She feels loved, wanted, like Biggie loves her more than he loves Tete. Yes, it is not fair on Tete, but he is too young for her.

The guilt still lingers, but it is getting less and less. She does worry, however, about the prospect of losing it all; the love of a boy, being wanted, being normal.

'What if aunty finds out about us?' she asks as she is lying in Biggie's arms, in Tete's bed for the umpteenth time.

Tete left about an hour ago, and will only come back in the afternoon to grab some lunch. With the light showers of rain pouring outside and it being still early in the morning, there is no chance of her coming back anytime soon.

'She won't,' says Biggie, 'unless you tell her.'

'Are you mad? But if she dares find out then we are dead. Dead, dead.'

'Stop talking like that. Look at the brighter side of life. That will never happen.'

Biggie is right?

Tete would never find out if Mercy was careful enough to not drop a packet of the pregnancy prevention pills in the bathroom two weeks ago, if Tete did not gladly pick these up and silently tuck them into her own handbag. They are not the same ones that she uses, and there could only be one other person using these in the house. 'Why does she need them?' she asked herself but was mature enough to keep this to herself, to not tip her off. Mercy did notice the missing pills of course, but because Tete did not say anything about it, as she was sure she would have if she'd found them, she is confident that they are somewhere in the house, that it is only a matter of time before she finds them. She did of course, when she missed them, search everywhere in her bedroom to no avail.

Biggie and Mercy still lying in bed, enveloped in the after-glory and listening to the sound of the rain softly hitting the asbestos roof, Tete enters the yard with her head covered with a hard plastic to shelter from the rain. She skips a few puddles near the road and in the middle of the small yard due to the poor drainage. She tiptoes to the door of the house in the back. Still unlocked as she left it, she opens the door and walks in, noiselessly, across the lounge. It does not take long for her to see the abomination on her bed since the bedroom door is wide open.

'Bastards!' she screams when she is still some two meters away from the door, picks up some shoes by the door and hurls them at the love birds.

There is not enough time for Biggie and Mercy to do anything else apart from opening their mouths in shock, Mercy hiding her face in her palms. Tete launches at them like a lioness, with fists and slaps and stilettos, and a jug full of water that she pours into their face. Mercy still naked, she cries and begs for forgiveness. Biggie battles to get dressed and to stop Tete from hitting his head with an electric iron. He knows that this is the end of the road for them, that he will be thrown out. He has dug his own grave.

'Biggie! Are you sure, Biggie?' Tete cries as she slumps into the corner of the room in a river of tears. 'I gave you everything, Biggie, everything. And this is how you pay me back, heh? With my niece, Biggie, my niece.'

He says nothing. Instead, he starts packing his clothes into a sports bag, hurriedly.

'And you, Mercy! My own child. Are you such a whore? I should have known. Stupid girl, today you and your deformed thing must leave my house. Back to the village.'

'I am sorry, aunty. It was uncle ...'

Getting up to her feet, Tete turns to Biggie, 'Leave my bag and my clothes. Everything that I bought, leave them. I look after you, I give you my whole self, everything. I picked you from the street and this is how you repay me? C'mon, leave my stuff, all of it...'

Biggie continues packing as Tete continues raging.

She grabs the bag and pulls out the clothes, all of which she bought since Biggie really bought nothing, even for himself, including the jeans and t-shirt now on his body. Mercy takes advantage of this tug-of-war to dress up and to pick up her son who has been crying next door for the past twenty minutes.

'Leave my things,' Tete fumes, grabbing Biggie's t-shirt and tearing it across the whole front. He lets go of the bag, snatches his phone from the charger and heads for the door.

'You too. I don't want to see you here. Leave my house now!' Tete screams at Mercy who is now sitting in the lounge.

'Where do I go, aunty?' she says as she kneels on the floor. 'Please have mercy on me.'

'Out! And leave the baby. You don't deserve him.' She grabs Tribulation away from her and nudges her forward with her knee. 'Follow your pimp. Bloody whore!'

Mercy storms out of the house in tears, wearing a mini-dress and with no shoes on her feet. When she hits the road the rain has stopped and several of their neighbours, having been alerted by the noise, are standing outside their houses, and a few others are milling by the gate, pointing and laughing. Biggie is walking hurriedly down the road, so she runs after him, splattering the water collected in the puddles on the edge of the road.

Eleven

MaNcube's story

He wouldn't be too worried if it were only himself to worry about. But, despite his insistence, she refuses to go back to Tete's house. She follows him around like a male termite tracking the pheromone of a female. Shoeless. When night comes, they are stranded around the Sakubva market, until he decides that they should try MaNcube's house which is located in the high-density suburb.

They are lucky when they arrive at the run-down compound in the middle of the night to find MaNcube still awake, sorting out her goods for sale at the mines tomorrow.

'You can put up here until you find a more suitable place,' she says after Biggie's explained the situation, leaving out a lot of detail and bending the facts.

'Thank you, *amai*, ah thank you,' he says.

'Thank you, *amai*,' Mercy repeats after him.

'No problem my children,' MaNcube says, then she looks at Mercy and smiles, 'He is like a child to me, your brother. When my son, my Mundewere, when he was still alive, they were always together like this. Like belt and trousers. But God decided it was time and he went, just like that, he went to join my father and mother and the multitude of the saints in the heavens. I know he made it into heaven because he was a good boy, he had a good heart, you know. Yes, he might have made mistakes here and there, but he was a good boy. I prayed for him every day.'

She seems to be struggling to justify why her son should have made it into the happily-ever-after, like she is not fully convinced he did.

'You are right, *amai*,' Biggie agrees. 'He was a good man, and good men go to heaven.'

He agrees although he doubts it, although he thinks that Mundewere would most likely be in hell, if indeed it exists, not heaven. He doesn't tell MaNcube about their escapades in the *shebeens,* where they prostituted themselves and outdid each other in the process. He doesn't tell her about how her son was so prolific that the name Mundewere was coined for him not because he could speak isiNdebele, but because of the bedroom noises which he expressed in fluent isiNdebele, complete with the clicks and tongue twisters despite the fact that he grew up in Manicaland. This became a hit with the prostitutes and over time spread around town until everyone began to call him Mundewere, to Shonalise it. His real name was Mthokozisi, but the whole town knew him as Mundewere.

'He told me all about that woman of yours,' she continues, now looking at Biggie, 'how she mistreated you and wanted to be the man of the house instead of being a good, compliant wife. I really don't know how you put up with her my son, so I am not surprised at all that she took another man and dumped you just like that, like the *iwule* that she is.'

'Forget about her, *amai*,' Biggie calms her down. 'Very soon my things will be back in shape, and my sister and I will be just fine.'

'You say you are from Rusape, my daughter?' she turns again to Mercy, who is startled and almost gives away the lie.

'Yes, *amai*,' she says as she looks down to the floor. She avoids saying too much and is embarrassed to be lying to this old woman like that, painting Tete with a brush dipped in tosh when it is Biggie and her that should be swimming in it. Quietly, she thinks about whether Tete would forgive her, if she goes back.

'Well,' continues MaNcube, 'one of my neighbours, Omega, is from Makoni. She lives just up the road. Maybe, if you settle in this area you can be friends and visit the village together, or you can send her with goods for your parents. I wish I had enough room here, but as you can see, since my boy left me I don't have much room to spare but this. My bedroom is full of all his stuff. I hope you understand. You can just sleep here, both of you, until the room is cleared. I will talk to the landlord tomorrow to let him know you are my guests.'

'Thank you, *amai*,' Biggie says. 'What would we have done without you? The world needs more people like you.'

In a few minutes, MaNcube leaves the two in the room as she retires to her bedroom, which is just next door. She has to first go out the door, onto the yard, in order to access the other room as the rooms are not adjoining despite being adjacent to each other. She is one of six tenants crammed at the property, of which there is no electricity supply. She occupies two rooms in the run-down, unpainted block of rooms built around what is supposed to be the main house, the original structure, which itself is in fact a single room joined together with the neighbours' own room in some form of terraced houses. The landlord, a Mr Wasu, is a retiree who worked for the railways many years ago, who used his pension lumpsum to build the many rooms scattered around the house in a haphazard fashion, obscuring the original core house (or room) which he uses as his own since he has no children. One can only tell apart the original structure because of it being joined to the neighbours'. And, because it is the last one on the block, at the corner, Mr

Wasu was able to build the many rooms around it, off plan, which were poorly built using farm bricks not properly cooked and were plastered with cement mixed with too much sand. They are susceptible to moulding during the rainy season, as is now, and the plastering is slowly crumbling down. The toilet and bathroom is a shared one, located just behind the houses, with at least five different addresses using the two structures, one for the men and the other for the women. It is a desperate existence, matched only by Matapi flats in Harare's Mbare suburb.

'You should go back to Tari and reason with her tomorrow,' Biggie suggests. 'You are her blood, she might just understand. Tribulation will need you.'

'Why did I do this?' Mercy asks herself, aloud, her eyes red.

Earlier, before coming to MaNcube's, they spent the day sitting around the market in Sakubva, thinking about their next move. It did cross Biggie's mind then, to just abandon her so she is forced to go back to Tete's house. But, having known Tete for so long, he decided that leaving Mercy alone would be tantamount to murder. The good side of him prevailed, so he decided to leave her with someone that she can share her burdens with, one who can be a mother to her. At the earliest opportunity, he would jump onto a *kombi* to Masvingo, and proceed to Bulawayo where he is sure he can make a living, somehow. He has never been to Bulawayo, but he knows it would give him the best chance of skipping the border into South Africa. That way he can run away from this stupid country and make a better living in *Mzansi*. He would probably find a decent Zulu woman to marry. This thought brought about a smile to his face, so much that Mercy wondered what went on in his head.

'Crying won't help,' Biggie informs her. 'We just have to look for a way out, use our brains.'

'Like what?'

'I don't know, but I will leave this town.'

'To go where?'

'Maybe to *Joza*. Some of my friends made it to *Joza* and they say it's *mnandi* there.'

'What about me, Biggie? Where do I go?' Mercy asks, looking into his eyes. He is serious. 'Do you want to leave me alone?'

'Unless you want to come with me,' he says, knowing very well that she would not agree to that, 'otherwise I don't have anything to give you in this city. Maybe you are better off going back to the village?'

'The village? No way. I can't go back there. *Nada*. I can't do that Biggie.'

'Why? Did something unpleasant happen there? You grew up there, so you can just go back.'

'I can't. I won't.'

That settles it. She won't go back to the village. She imagines what life would be like if she were to do that, a mother with a disabled child, without a husband. What would the village people say when they get wind of what happened between her and Tete? No, she can't go back there.

It is raining again outside, with thunder and lightning. The heavy showers hit against the metal roof like someone is pouring a flurry of pebbles onto it. Water begins dripping through, and finally pouring through, the many holes in the roof, wetting the cloth that is spread on the concrete floor, making two sides of the room uninhabitable. They hurdle together in the middle of the room, underneath the single blanket MaNcube gave them. They are hungry. They have not eaten anything the whole day and there is nothing to eat in the room. MaNcube keeps her food in her bedroom, except for the maize meal which is on the lower tray of the brown push-tray, and the tin of salt which is on the top tray, next to the paraffin stove.

They are in Sakubva for a few weeks, living from hand to mouth. Every morning, Biggie goes to the terminus as usual, but this time he demands more money from the drivers. He pretty much declares the terminus his own, forcing the drivers and other *hwindis* to pay him in order to use it. It works. He makes a bit of money, and brings some of it to the house, to MaNcube and Mercy. MaNcube is happy. She feels like she has regained her son, that Mundewere has come back to her. They even eat *sadza* with more than greens, with bones which they buy at the market, after MaNcube returns from selling her wares in the gold mines near the town. She goes there every weekday, although she doesn't come near the Chiadzwa diamond mines. People are dying there, chased away and killed by the army and the Chinese, who are clandestinely exploiting the gems. She could make more money there, but it is too risky.

Mercy does try to go back to Tete's house, but every time she finds her not at home. Finally, she visits her market stall in town, and there, she is undressed by Tete in public, and insulted by all her friends. They throw hurtful words at her: prostitute, husband-snatcher, scum-of-the-earth. Crying does not change anything. When she learns that Tete dumped Tribulation in the village, she decides that she has no more reason to beg her for anything. She has to survive on her own.

Biggie's success at the terminus gives them hope. It lasts until the municipality police descends on the terminus and rounds up the *hwindis*, accusing them of lawlessness. Biggie is forced to retreat and stay at the house. He sulks every day.

Mercy wakes up in the morning and realises that he is gone, the little bag in which he kept his clothes with him. It is clear that she has been deserted, that she and MaNcube are back to scavenging.

'He will come back,' MaNcube says. 'He is a good boy.'

'I don't think so, *amai*,' says Mercy. 'I thought things were now looking up for us, then this.'

This time she doesn't cry. She is tired of it. She has to pull up her socks and do something. Survive.

'Don't worry my daughter. You can just come with me to the mines. The two of us can stay here, together, and with our combined effort, we can make a difference.'

'My life is a mess, *amai*, so messed up.'

'Don't say that my daughter. Who knows what God has in store for us tomorrow? You might just get married to a rich man, who knows, with all that beauty it could just happen.'

Mercy shakes her head in disagreement. The old woman is too hopeful. She doesn't know the story of her life. Marriage is not possible for her. Nothing can deliver her from this suffering.

'You should come to church with me. There are some fine young men there,' MaNcube continues. 'Yes, that's the solution that you need. You need God.'

'To come to church to look for a husband, *amai*? I don't think your God would want that from his worshippers.'

'That is not what I meant. But you have to position yourself, you know. Men will not come to this stupid house looking for you. You have to position yourself well, that is what our mothers taught us. And it worked. If it were not for my husband's people who disliked me just because I am Ndebele, things had worked nicely for me.'

'What happened, *amai*?' Mercy is now curious. 'What happened to you?'

'It is a long story my daughter,' she begins. 'His name is Moses, but I called him Mozy. He owns a big supermarket in Harare which I hear is running very well, even to this day.

141

I even went to see him when I heard he was doing very well. I thought that he would be interested in taking care of his son. And I think he was. But the wife, ey, she looked at me like she was seeing poop. Dog's poop. I never heard back from him. It is not his wife's fault though. It is because of the people of this region, these Manyika people; you see them like this, but they are very evil. They chased me like a dog when Mozy brought me as the woman he wanted to marry. They said that Ndebele women are prostitutes, can you imagine? And he listened to them, his family, and he dumped me just like that, with a child. His child.'

'I am sorry,' Mercy says, in a pitiful voice.

'No. Don't feel sorry for me. Yes, life has not been kind to me, but God has been. He knows what he is doing. Job suffered more than this.'

'If you say so, *amai*.'

Her story is heart-wrenching enough, so she agrees to come with her to the church. It is a newly formed Pentecostal one, sweeping the country like a wild fire, miracles and fire said to be raining all over the place. The branch in Sakubva is the most known in the region. It claims a number of young people as part of its congregation, with a band that plays more *sungura* music than the old-time hymns, and a pastor who preaches as if he is to bring down the old building with his voice. The other pastors, those of the traditional churches that have been in existence for a long time, do not like this new gospel that promises people *utopia* and is robbing them of their membership. They preach against the new church from all pulpits, but it seems like the more they do this the more the church expands. MaNcube is one of the faithful, so when she introduces Mercy, the pastor, who never misses a new congregant, is very happy to see her.

'I like your church, *amai*,' she says afterwards. 'It is not like the one in the village.'

'You see. I knew you would like it.'

Twelve

Once bitten

They ek out a living by hitting the mines and the gold panning places along the river for days, with dishes on their heads loaded with soap and cigarettes and sugar and powdered milk, encouraging the miners to spend their hard earned dough on the essentials. If the timing of their visit is right, that is at the end of the week when the miners are paid their wages, the items are grabbed away promptly. They are especially there Thursday afternoons so they can also collect their dues from those miners who oftentimes take stuff on credit, giving one excuse or another, and are a pain to collect from at the end of the week as they vanish into thin air to run after the opaque beer, *masese*, only resurfacing days after the money is finished.

Mercy proves to be a hit with the men at the mines. They all seem eager to try their luck with the beauty, but they always hit a brick wall, one after the other. Now she guards herself jealously, much more like when she was back at the village and no boy dared come close to her, when she was famed for not giving in to the older boys and male teachers who oftentimes crossed the line because they just couldn't stop themselves. It was only Freedom that she was smitten with, eventually, but with clear limits that included 'no touching.' She and Chipo prided themselves in having been able to keep themselves clean despite many of their agemates having lost their virginity to the older boys and men when they were as young as thirteen.

'You have to wait until you get married,' Mother advised her many times. 'Rushing will only hurt you in the long run.'

Her advice rang loud and clear each time the boys approached her, so she removed herself from them as far as she could. Besides, Father would have killed her if she were to do as little as get a boyfriend before she finished school. Mother would also lose her RW status if she were to get pregnant outside of marriage. So, Freedom was truly an exception. He had come to the school from Harare when they were in Form Two, and he was much older as he had previously flanked his O Levels. His father had then wheeled him back three classes to as far back as Form Two, which he could only do at the rural school in a sort of punishment that was meant to make him realise that life is not soft. He stayed with his grandparents and was an instant hit with the girls at the school. Clever and mature, he knew enough to not call the pretty girl before she called him first. It did not take time for him to notice that none of the boys dared come close to the pretty one; one, because of her parents, and two, because whoever tried ended up with blood in their face after she head-butted them with her principled 'no', going as far as reporting the pesters to VaMusungwa who would unsparingly dish the lazy boys a good canning in their backsides. He waited until they were in the last term of Form Two and he had set himself apart as the nice one, the disinterested one. Thus, he found himself going to Mother's church and sitting as far away from Mercy as possible, but where she could see him.

One day he greeted her, simply, when she was alone and Chipo was not with her. 'Hello,' he said.

'Hello,' she replied. He meant well.

'You seem to be so dedicated to the church ...'

'Of course, I am. My Mother heads the RW.'

'I know. Only a few people are as dedicated as you ...'

'Do you want to help me fetch water for the reverend?' she asked, not allowing him to finish his sentence and beginning to walk away.

He followed behind, trotting.

She didn't know then that she liked him, not only because he was good looking, but because all the girls in her class liked him too. They had all at one time, with the exception of Chipo and her, tried to impress him. So, she was not ignorant of the fact that his talking to her was in some way an honour, something the other girls would kill for. She was not, however, ready for her record of breaking hearts to be broken by anyone, not even this Freedom. She didn't even realise that he was pursuing her, until she found herself spending a lot of time with him at the school and he walked her home every day, leaving her somewhere close to the cattle pens which are a few meters away from the homestead. Until she found herself eating her lunch with him, sitting next to him in class and missing him when he was not there. In fact, he never asked her out officially. He was clever enough to not solicit for the 'no.' It was clear to the other boys and girls, including to Chipo, that the lioness had been tamed and was soon to be slaughtered. Freedom would lift the trophy.

Mother did suspect that something was cooking when she found them always together at the church, sitting next to each other, but instead of asking she decided to advise. 'You realise that these boys you meet at church are not your real brothers, right?' she asked. Mercy knew what she meant, so she assured her that she would always remember that.

Then Chipo acquired her own boyfriend, Lovemore, and when she broke it to her she did not object. 'Well, I think we are now big enough to have boyfriends,' she said. That settled it. Chipo with Lovemore, Mercy with Freedom. It became their identity in the school, and still Freedom never asked, he just went about telling the boys of his conquest and they all believed him. The evidence was clear. And of course, Freedom's love for church slowly diminished, and the wings began to grow.

'You have proved to be a winner for the business,' MaNcube says as they wait patiently by the makeshift gate of one of the gold mines.

A yellow digger drives through the gate, which is manned by a big black man originally from Zambia, slowly.

'How?' she asks.

'Of course, all these people flock to us not because they want to buy our stuff, but to see you. That never used to happen ...'

It doesn't make her feel comfortable.

'What do they want from me?' she asks. 'Do you think I look like an easy girl to them?'

'No, my daughter. You are just beautiful, pretty, that's all. They would all die to have you. Just look at them carefully, each of them, none wants any of the things that they buy, they just find themselves doing so when you smile and talk to them. None of them would do if it were not because of you. You see, men are just but animals, most of the time. That thing between their legs, sometimes it controls them and turns them into little babies.'

Mercy laughs, heartily. 'I think you are stretching it a bit, *amai*. They are just wasting their time with me anyway.'

'Yes, you are right. Never give in to any of these *brakwachas*. You deserve better. Let them die with want if they will, let their manhoods explode. But in the meantime, it's all good business for us.'

They laugh their hearts out, just as the siren goes off and in a few minutes the men and women in dusty overalls pour out of the gate. The hawkers camped at the gate ready their stuff for sale. Most of them do sweets and fruits as the miners are provided with cooked food on site, which is delivered in huge aluminium pots and pans and is served piping hot.

'MaNcu, the beauty from Matabeleland,' one of the miners exclaims. 'MaNcu, the one who doesn't get old. What did you bring for me this time?'

'Well, nothing for you since you still haven't paid for my cigarettes from last time,' she says, 'but for others, of course, there is plenty of stuff here. Look.'

'No, no, MaNcube, please. You can't embarrass me in front of your beautiful daughter like this. I am not a bad person at all. I make good money here and very soon I will be the foreman in there. Look, I have even brought your money.'

He reaches into his pockets and draws out a bundle of old bearer cheques, which is now the currency in use due to hyperinflation. He counts another bundle out of these and hands it over to MaNcube. 'You see now. No need to embarrass me,' he continues, beaming.

They all come in that fashion, mobbing MaNcube and Mercy and causing the other hawkers, who are mainly men and not-so-gifted women, to burn with envy. They are jealous, but they can't do anything apart from cursing under their breath. They are happier when MaNcube and Mercy are not there as they would be able sell much of their own stuff.

For what seems to be days without end, Mercy hits the mines with her new mother, hoarding stuff from the CBD, a few times bumping into Tete in the CBD and turning away from her to avoid a confrontation. She also bumps into a few other people from the village, on occasion, who visit the market for different reasons. They keep her updated of the different developments in the village, of the forced political meetings at Chief Chisindi's compound, and of Nurse Mupunga's new status as leader of the RW. Nurse Mupunga is said to be doing much better than Mother, despite Mother having sworn that the RW would never be the same without her. Melusi is said to have been in the district hospital for a long time, and Mapudege now dwells at the district growth-point where she cooks *sadza* and sells it to revellers at one of the many bottle-stores there. Chipo is doing a nursing course at the hospital, thanks to the generosity of Reverend Mbudzi. Lovemore, on the other hand, is said to have relocated to the previously white commercial farming district where he is working as a general hand. It is over between him and Chipo.

The stories from the village fascinate her. She imagines the different places there, how they might have changed and how some of the younger children should all be grown up now. She deliberately avoids talking about Tribulation, and about Mother and Father. She doesn't want the picture that they bring to her mind, what they remind her of, of the suffering and misfortune that she associates with them. One day, she thinks, she will have enough and she will go back to the dirty village and pull her son out of it.

'We are late for church,' MaNcube says on a Sunday. 'Pastor Munamato is preaching again today. He seems to like you a lot, and when you don't go he always asks after you.'

'*Amai*, you and your hopes again. That man will never come near a pig like me.'

'Don't say that my daughter. You are fearfully and wonderfully made in the image of God.'

Mercy laughs, as if to say, 'I don't believe you.'

'Let's rush then,' she says instead as she locks the door from the outside, clipping the huge chain with the trunk lock.

Munamato is still a trainee pastor although he preaches most of the time these days. Pastor Jonathan is grooming him. Raised up in Mutoko, he came to Mutare Teachers' College to further his studies with the aim of afterwards pursuing a career as a secondary school teacher. He came to the church, Fire Rain Ministries, when he was still a student at the college, after he felt the fire burn in him so much that he could not wait anymore. After he felt that he was meant to be in full time ministry and not teaching, that if he did not pay attention to this fire he would be consumed by it. Not wanting to be like the biblical Jonah, he left his teaching training after a few months and joined the ministry on a full-time basis. Pastor Jonathan introduced him to Bishop Ndoro, who enrolled him into the bible school in Harare.

Six months after completing his training, Munamato is back in town preaching like the world will end tomorrow, drawing in huge swarms of people, young and old, who cling to his words as if they would drop dead if they didn't. He is swimming in the glory and doesn't at all regret having left his teaching job. After all, how much does a teacher earn these days if not but peanuts, if many of them are fleeing to neighbouring countries in order to earn a decent wage? Clearly, he is better off as a pastor than as a poor chalk-breaker.

'Amen!' the congregants respond in unison to Munamato's fiery message about walking in tune with the Holy Ghost.

MaNcube is up on her feet and dancing and jumping up and down with the rest of them. Mercy sits there, quietly enjoying the atmosphere. She is still trying to come to grips with this way of worship although she does feel somewhat uplifted in her spirit when she is there. Her pain just lifts up like grease dissolved in a powerful chemical and she finds herself wrapped up in a beautiful cloud of hope, at least for this moment, like one who is totally stoned. Dressed in a white blouse, long light blue skirt and flat shoes and her hair having been properly done by the famed hairdresser of Sakubva, it would be impossible for any boy with living worms inside their crotch not to take notice of her.

It is not surprising that after the church service, when Munamato is standing by the door greeting people and telling them 'God bless you and have a wonderful week' in a sweet voice, that when it is Mercy and MaNcube's turn he engages them for a longer time, ignoring the people who have pretty much queued up to greet him. MaNcube, discerning as she is, excuses herself to allow the two more time. Who knows what could come out of this, she thinks.

Having been pre-warned by MaNcube and having already noticed the young pastor's interest, Mercy is shy to be left talking to him alone. Besides, she really doesn't know the man. Her sceptical, injured self stands erect inside her soul, ready to defend.

'You should come to the youth meetings during the week,' Munamato suggests.

'I will be working then, but I will try when I am free.'

'Please do. I would be happy to see you there. A lot.'

'Yes, pastor.'

'No. Listen. This 'pastor' tag puts a barrier between servants of God and the people. You and I, we are the same, we are all saints, so no need to call me pastor all the time.'

She thinks it weird that he asks her that, since all other people call him by the title. Even Reverend Mbudzi, she calls him 'reverend', not by his first name.

He smiles and she melts. 'Yes, pastor,' she says.

'Maybe I was not clear,' he says, not smiling. 'You are free to call me Munamato, truly; that is my name. Right, Mercy?'

'Yes pastor, eh, Munamato.'

'That's right. Have a blessed week.'

'Yes, pastor,' she says as she begins to walk away, as he turns around to greet and talk to the other congregants who are still milling around, with much more happiness.

Munamato is not the only one who has taken notice of the angel. A few of the brothers have also seen the glory.

In the following weeks and months, she receives a lot of suitors and is confused as to what it all means, whether any or all or none of it mean anything. She is now very much scared of men, having landed herself into trouble because of Biggie and having gone through that ordeal with Father. She feels that she hates all men, that they are dogs as Mother once said. Now she understands why Tete is still not married. Like Biggie said, marriage is not for everyone. There are very few men out there who are after anything other than planting their thingy inside a woman. After all, if Father could be as dishonourable as he was, then surely no man can be trusted. So, unbeknown to the brothers who stampede over each other to try and get a date with and to try and impress her, her heart is pretty much closed. Besides, never in her life has she said 'yes' to any man, not even to Freedom. Getting these words out of her would require some dedicated mining.

They come to her with all sorts of stories, the brothers, from glorious heavenly visions God has shown them about their future with her, as many as they are, to threats about disobeying the Holy Ghost and risking a curse from God if she dares to say no. She is too confused at the end of it all and decides, rationally, that she will have to face whatever God brings to her, as long as she does not pay attention to these absurdities.

MaNcube continues to encourage her.

In the end, she does go to the mid-week youth meetings, but, being very much aware of Munamato's interest, she tries by all means to steer away from him, giving all sorts of excuses.

Her problem, however, is Tinashe, who is the only one of her many suitors who looks and sounds different. He is tall and slim and soft spoken and does not come to her with heavenly glorious visions and voices shouting 'she is the one I have given over to you my dear son.' She likes him. He reminds her of her Freedom, in the old days before he started growing wings. She thinks that he is worth of giving a chance, although she won't make it any easier for him. He has to work for it if he truly wants it.

'Why are you turning away every boy that comes to you, even Tinashe?' MaNcube asks. 'He comes here and does not seem to care that you come from this dirty place. Why not give the young man a chance?'

'Iii, *amai*, these boys are all the same. They pretend that they have fallen head over heels for you, but as soon as they get what they really want, you won't see them ever again.'

'You are too cautious, Mercy. Do not let your past dictate your future. The mistakes that you made should not hold you captive ...'

'I know, *amai*, but you know that is better said than done.'

She does consider Tinashe's advances after this, opening up to him about her Tribulation, but not about Father or Biggie. He loves her still. He is happy to live with whatever past she has, to be a father to Tribulation. She is about to let him in when Munamato comes out of the blue and stirs up the muddy waters one more time.

There is no more hiding for her, she has to decide between Munamato and Tinashe. With Tinashe, she feels the attraction, and he is the better-looking one. With Munamato, there is security: she would become *Mai Mufundisi*, the pastor's wife, like Mrs Mbudzi. A Man of God, it also means she can bank on his word.

When she tells Tinashe her final answer and reveals to him that she is now in a relationship with Munamato, he is crashed. He cries as he sits in MaNcube's room, begging her to reverse her decision. He is unsuccessful.

'I can go to bible school if that's what you want,' he pleads.

'I am sorry,' Mercy replies, 'but I am only one person. I have made my decision.'

Her heart is bleeding on the inside.

'You are a good man, Tinashe, and you deserve a better wife, much better than me,' she adds. 'There are plenty of girls out there who would die to have a man like you.'

Many days go by and despite her efforts, Tinashe does not go away. He continues to bog her, directly and indirectly, even when she feels that she is falling deeply in love with Munamato, who turns out to be not a bad guy after all. She really wants it to work between them. He takes her all over the place, parading her as the pastor's future wife, in the process resuscitating her heart which was almost dying, causing her to believe in love again. What more with him telling her that their union was ordained in heaven, that he knew from the first time he set his eyes on her that she was the one God reserved for him, she knows that all her misfortune thus far was meant to strengthen her. It will soon be buried and forgotten. She reads her bible more.

Even Pastor Jonathan thinks that they are a match made in heaven. Theirs is now the model relationship for the youths in the church. A bright future lies ahead. Once again, Mercy finds herself at that point where her life is set to change for the better. A turning point.

Thirteen

Man of God

There is probably some truth in the notion that Adam had already succumbed to the temptation long before Eve invited him to partake of the forbidden fruit in the middle of the garden. His eyes must have already flirted with and been seduced by the delicious fruit that it was easy for him to forget the Lord's clear instruction and give in to the serpent's craftiness.

Munamato is very much aware of that.

The open-air gospel crusade in Nyanga, where he preached, was a resounding success, with bumper crowds which exceeded all expectations. He is proud of having shared the platform with other preachers from around the world, in order to win lost souls for the kingdom. They were all so impressed with how easily he captured people's attention. They are all talking about him.

'Well done, Man of God,' Pastor Jonathan says to him. 'God has used you, mightily.'

'It is by God's grace, pastor,' he replies, humbly.

'Keep the fire burning my brother. The word says that he who puts his hand to the plough and looks back is not fit for the kingdom. You have begun well, so you will finish well.' Pastor Jonathan lays his right hand upon his head as he speaks these words, as the other pastors and their wives agree with him by nodding their heads and saying 'Amen'.

They are in the dining area of the beautiful Troutbeck Inn hotel, overlooking the lake.

'I receive it, pastor,' says Munamato, bowing his head and lifting up his hands like a soldier surrendering to the enemy on the field of war.

'It is well with you my brother, it is well.'

'It is well.'

Mercy is proud of her husband-to-be, so she thanks God for his favour upon her life. She sleeps like a baby despite being tired from the crusade where she was an usher, running around and helping those who needed help. She and Munamato sleep in different rooms as they are not yet married, after he kisses her hand and says 'Good night, darling,' and Pastor Jonathan smiles at the sight of it.

In the morning, they wake up early and take with them packed breakfast. Pastor Jonathan, Bishop Ndoro and their wives drive to Harare in the bishop's 4x4 Land Cruiser, whilst Munamato drives the Fire Rain pick-up truck, which is normally used Pastor Jonathan, back to Mutare with Mercy.

The idea of branching off to see Tribulation in the village is not Mercy's. Munamato is keen to see where she comes from, although he will have to be careful not to get into Father's presence since he has not yet paid *lobola*. He will stay at the village centre and she will bring Tribulation there.

They negotiate the bumpy dusty road which has not been maintained for ages, either due to the district council's complacency or, as is most likely the case, due to the funds meant for this having been squandered by the clever ones. The people will again be promised 'better roads' in the next election, during which a little stretch of the road will be mend as a sign of the politicians' commitment.

The truck leaves behind a cloud of dust as Munamato speeds across the dangerous terrain like he has had a pint of testosterone injected into him.

'Don't kill us, please,' Mercy begs him.

'Don't worry. The Holy Ghost is in control,' he says. 'Besides, dying is fast track to heaven.'

'Iii, please, some of us still want to live right here on earth.'

They are busy having a good laugh when one of the tyres hits a rock and picks up a sharp metal object which sinks into and flattens it completely. Munamato battles to keep the truck on the slippery road before stopping on the side of the road, on a bend.

'Jesus!' he exclaims as they both immediately open their doors and dash out to look at the damage.

'It's completely done,' he says, 'and we don't have a spare.'

'So, what are you going to do?'

'I don't know. I can try taking it out and hope that someone comes along who can take it to the growth-point for repair.'

'Oh no. We shouldn't have come this way,' says Mercy. She thinks that maybe the spirits of the land are against her, that her coming back to the village is the cause of their misfortune.

'Come, help me,' says Munamato as he grabs the toolbox from the back of the seat and lies flat underneath the vehicle, facing upwards, to position the jack. He spreads the jacket of one of his many suits onto the damp surface.

In a few minutes the wheel is out, but they have nowhere to go as it is in the middle of nowhere, surrounded by trees and rocks. The next village is a few miles ahead and Mercy is fully aware of how infrequently the road is used. It could be hours before another vehicle comes by. They sit on the side of the road, eating apples and crisps which they grabbed with their breakfast from the hotel.

The seconds tick on until they are minutes and the minutes almost an hour, yet still no vehicle comes along, except for a motorbike which is going in the opposite direction and would really not be of any assistance to them.

'I can't help you, I am sorry,' says the biker, putting back his helmet and cranking the motorbike to restart it. 'What I could do is call my friend who is a mechanic when I am somewhere I can pick up a signal. But it will be at least an hour before he turns up.'

'Thanks my brother,' says Munamato. 'God will bless you. We will wait for your friend.'

After a few directions from Munamato, the man rides on.

It makes sense for them to wait for the mechanic, even if another vehicle comes along. Thus, after they lock the doors and position the yellow and red triangle a bit further away from the truck, they cross the road and go up the hill where they sit on some rocks, basking in the early sunshine as the sun climbs up over the eastern mountains and direct its rays towards them through the trees.

They are relaxed and comfortable when they begin to mess around. First is a pat on the shoulder, arms around the waist, then a kiss on the mouth. Before they know it, they are fornicating on the rocks, against the moral standards of the church. It is only after they are done that the small little voice becomes louder, that they realise what they have done, just like Adam and Eve realised their nakedness only after their master had called in the garden. Mercy is particularly ashamed of herself for having dropped the ball again.

Munamato assures her that it shouldn't be any matter since she is going to be his wife anyway, hence strictly speaking and according to him, it really is not a sin.

'And when is it that you are going to marry me?' she questions.

'Soon. Very soon.'

It does give her some peace, the answer, but she is still a little confused. She thinks that the pastor should have had more control, that he should have known better. MaNcube certainly wouldn't approve of such, she thinks, so she won't tell her about this as she seems to be too devoted than the Man of God. After all, he is the pastor and she is the disciple, so if it is okay for him it should definitely be okay for her too. They will get married, properly, and the thought of it makes her smile. She pictures herself in a pure white dress and Munamato in an equally white suit, with lots of confetti floating in the air and jubilant singing from the Fire Rain choir. It helps diffuse the guilt; she feels it lift away, and she feels much better than that time with Biggie. Not only that, but the pictures of Father sweating on top of her did not at all flash across her mind like they did then. It must be a good sign, she thinks.

'We should get going,' Munamato interrupts her thoughts.

When they get back to the vehicle they find the mechanic waiting for them in his Mazda truck which is parked just behind theirs. He has brought with him a good spare wheel and adhesives to try and mend theirs. After a few words with Munamato they agree that it is better to just use the new tyre instead of mending the other.

As they are still talking by the side of the road, Reverend Mbudzi's truck approaches, going in the opposite direction. He is about to pass them when he notices Mercy and applies the breaks.

'I can't believe that I am seeing you, Mercy,' he says as he gets out of the vehicle and crosses over to their side of the road.

'Reverend,' she says. 'Good to see you.'

'Look at you. City life is good hey, even the skin has changed …'

'Don't say that, reverend. I miss home so much,' she says, lying.

'Hello, sir,' Munamato greets the reverend, firmly as if to announce his presence.

'Hello, young man. Are you travelling together with my daughter?'

'Yes, sir,' he says, shaking his hand.

'He is my boyfriend, and he is a pastor.'

'Pastor. Oh, I see. I am glad to see that you have not forsaken the Lord my daughter. So, how are you staying in the village?'

'Not long at all, we will be going back today. How is Chipo?'

'She is doing fine. If all goes well she will graduate this year.'

'Glad to hear that.'

After a few words, Reverend Mbudzi goes on his way, and in a few minutes, Munamato and Mercy are on their way, reaching the village centre well after midday. Munamato parks the vehicle under the big mango tree and takes a stroll as Mercy makes a dash to her father's homestead. She greets a few people at the village centre before she heads off. They are all excited to see her and they keep looking at Munamato and the parked vehicle with curiosity.

Mother and Tribulation are in the fields when she gets to the homestead, and Father is mending the kitchen's thatching, laying on new bundles of brown grass and tying it with ropes made from the buck of the *mutondo* tree.

'Welcome, my daughter,' Father says as he climbs down the ladder, just as she enters the yard. 'Do you bring good news? Is everything alright where you are coming from?'

'Yes, *baba*,' she says as she proceeds to Mother in the fields, who is now up from her bending position and is looking at her in disbelief, the little hoe that she is busy cutting withered maize stalks with in her hand. She puts the hoe down and runs to embrace with her daughter, the two of them almost falling over Tribulation. Mother has lost a lot of weight.

'Are you okay, *mama*?' Mercy asks.

Mother does not reply. She is crying. She wraps her arms around her one more time. 'My daughter, my daughter,' she cries. 'I thought we would never see you again, that you would never come back to us.'

'I am not staying, *mama*,' she says as she picks up Tribulation from the dust. He is now a big boy, but his shorter leg is now thinner. He cannot stand on his own for more than a couple of minutes, so he moves around by dragging his body along the ground. He seems to not recognise Mercy.

'Why?' Mother asks as they begin to walk towards the compound.

'Do you remember me, Tribe?' Mercy says as she tries to charm Tribulation. He doesn't respond, but looks at Mother and says, '*Mama*.'

'He doesn't remember me, *mama*,' she says with tearful eyes. 'I am sorry my son, I am sorry. I am your mother, Tribe, do you not remember me?'

She wipes the tears and tries to control her emotions. Tribulation looks at her and wonders, then he starts crying in a hoarse voice, quietly at first and vehemently when he realises that she is not letting go of him. '*Mama*,' he cries for Mother until she hands him over to her.

'Don't worry, my daughter. He will get used, it will all come back to him.'

Mercy is sad as they walk into the yard.

'You still haven't told me why you have to go back today?' Mother continues.

'I have a friend, *mama*, and he is waiting for me at the shops. He drove me here and wants us to go back today,' she explains.

'So, why did you leave him there, alone? Is it Biggie?' asks Mother.

'No, *mama*! Don't talk about Biggie. His name is Munamato, and he is a pastor.'

'A pastor?' Mother's face shines brighter. 'Is he your boyfriend?'

'Yes, and he wants to marry me.'

Mother begins to cry again, as if she is battling some demons.

'Stop crying,' Mercy says as they sit down in the shade of the tree on the edge of the homestead, joining Father.

Mother wipes off her tears and, after the traditional greetings, Mercy tells them all about Munamato, how good a man he is. They are all smiles by the time she takes Tribulation with her to the shops to see him. He is too heavy for her to carry, so she pushes him in a wheelbarrow for the short distance, his head and back resting against a pillow. He still doesn't talk to her, but looks at her with quizzing eyes.

At the end of the day, when she leaves the village, having retuned Tribulation back to Mother, she is loaded with a sack full of beans, groundnuts, cut sugar cane and several goodies. Her journey to the village, after all, has not been as bad as she imagined. Her only regret is that she didn't get to see Chipo, to explain herself and to try and resuscitate their friendship.

Fourteen

Rude awakening

For many months, he doesn't call or visit. The voice messages which she leaves him every time, after the phone has rung and rung and the sweet female voice has said 'please leave a message', have pretty much fallen onto deaf ears. Even after she tells him of MaNcube's illness in several text messages, still there is no response. Pastor Jonathan is not helpful either, he provides very little information and professes ignorance of his whereabouts. 'I have four pastors here, and the work is growing. Munamato has his own work to worry about in Harare,' he says.

'But, pastor . .?'

'I am sorry, Mercy, but you are the one that was in a relationship with him, not me.'

She tries to be calm, convincing herself that there should be a good reason why Munamato hasn't been back to see her, why he has not communicated the way he used to. It surely must be a slip of the tongue when Pastor Jonathan speaks of their relationship in past tense. The suggestion that, after sleeping with her for months, the pastor has bailed on his promise to marry her, cannot be entertained. She can't at this moment have been dumped again as if she were some sack of potatoes, a football kicked about by the ghetto kids of Sakubva. If he does that to her, God forbid, she would surely hunt him down and find him, and pluck out his balls like Chipo said, with her bare fingers.

'Munamato is an honourable man,' MaNcube reassures her from her bed of sickness. Her coughing is now so bad that those passing on the street can hear it when she starts. It is dry and hoarse. One can feel her chest tear apart. Mercy and Omega stay by her side most of the time, begging her to gobble the various pills which they buy from unlicensed hawkers in the Sakubva market. MaNcube drinks them all, one by one, throughout the day. Pastor Jonathan has been to see her and to pray for her once, a long time ago, but she has not seen him again since that time. She doesn't hold it against him, however. Rather, she holds on to her bible, which she places against her chest in an open position all the time when she is lying on her back, and which she tucks underneath her pillow when she turns to sleep on her side.

'Mercy,' she says in a whisper.

'*Amai.*'

'Whatever happens to me, do not worry yourself. If I go, I go, I will meet with my saviour. Just tell the church and they will see what they can do. Live your life. You still have a long way to go, my daughter... And Munamato, I know in my heart that he is a good man. He will come back for you.'

'Yes, *amai.*'

She is careful to not worry her, but she is troubled and now thinking of visiting Munamato in Harare. She will visit the mines alone and save a little money, and she will ask Omega to accompany her to Harare since she has never been to the big city all her life. They will go on a Sunday so they can be sure to find him at the church. Omega is streetwise. She seems to know everything despite her wallowing in the poverty of Sakubva.

'Not a problem, *munin'ina,*' Omega says when Mercy tells her of the plan, 'as long as you provide the money for transport.'

'Do you think he will be happy to see me?'

What she wants is assurance, but Omega does not do that. She is a straight talker.

'If he loves you, maybe. But as there really is no such thing as love, I doubt it. You see, love is just a wonderful concept to make life liveable, to massage people so they can tolerate the pain of living together. It is only for two reasons that people get married: to appease society and to make babies, and it is for these very same reasons that they stay together, even after they realise that those that advised them were just kidding. No love there. But, of course you church-people live in this fantasyland where people can be trusted and everything is fine. I am sorry to disappoint you, *munin'ina,* but me thinks that there is a good chance this pastor of yours has moved on. He's probably hooked up with a new concubine under the bright lights of Harare.'

Mercy hates Omega's forthrightness. She concludes, inside her own head, that Omega doesn't fully understand the love between Munamato and her. She doesn't understand that her lover is a pastor, one whose boss is none other than God himself. He is not some random boy from the ghetto. She didn't expect any real advice from Omega, anyway, given her dubious character.

'You are always critical of church-people, Omega. Why?' she asks.

'I am older than you Mercy, much older. I have seen enough. That's why. When I want a churchman, for whatever reason, I just go see them and they give me what I want. You see. They pray for me, and that is where it ends.'

'So, you do actually believe in God?'

'Of course, I do. Everybody does,' she says. 'The problem is you and your Munamato kind of people, who want to personalise God. As for me, I would rather go to *mapostori*, no strings attached. You see, *mapostori* just lay their hands on you and give you real answers, as long as you pay of course.'

'Iii, my sister. I will not comment on that.'

In the weeks that follow, she is in the mines every day, except for Sundays when she is at Fire Rain, and she saves every dollar she makes, apart from what she uses for MaNcube's pills and food.

The good and bad thing about time, is that it always comes to pass, whether or not you like it, whether or not you take heed. Faithfully, the sun rises and sets, days are added to the calendar, and young babies grow older and draw closer to a full understanding of what it means to be dead, of knowing whether or not there really is another life beyond the grave.

Mercy and Omega are on the ZUPCO bus to Harare, at the break of dawn, on their way to that place of reckoning where it will all be settled, where it will be established what it is that has caused the back to ache. What it is that has kept the good pastor holed up in the sunshine city despite his undying love for his beautiful future wife.

By the time the sun is up, they are already past Rusape. Next stop, Marondera. Omega is in blue tight jeans, a white armless t-shirt and a jean jacket. Mercy is in her long blue skirt, a white blouse and a woollen jersey in cream, befitting of a pastor's wife-to-be. She is just as hopeful as she is apprehensive.

'Are you sure it is alright, what we are doing?' Omega asks.

'Why?'

'Stalking a man. That is what we are doing.'

'A man who promised to marry me ...'

'What if he has moved on, what will you do?'

'No. He can't do that,' she shakes her head.

'Sure, he can. It's not like he was ever married to you,' Omega insists.

'But he... he promised to marry me... he slept with me.'

'Well, we will see, but as the older one here, I just need to warn you, that you should budget for disappointment. This is life. It is never fair ...'

The words sink right into her as she leans against Omega's shoulder in the largely empty bus. There are about ten other people on the bus, apart from them, all men and one woman who has a child of about three years of age, who cries after every two minutes in spite of her efforts to quieten him. The men are pretty much annoyed by it.

'Why don't you put the damn baby to sleep?' says one of the men, who has a long beard and a brown hat, loudly. He is sitting just behind the woman.

'Yes,' concurs another, who is on the adjacent seat. 'Are you enjoying the child's crying, woman? What's wrong with you?'

The woman doesn't respond, but holds the young boy in her arms and rocks him as he kicks about frantically and tries to spring himself free from her grasp. 'Stop doing that, Tindo,' she finally snaps in anger, frustrated. The boy is even more excited, so when she lets go of him, he runs along the passage of the bus and knocks over one old man's walking stick which was rested against the seat. She follows behind and grabs him by the arm, then slaps him hard across the face. He knocks his head against the seat and, after what looked like a long pause with his mouth wide open, the loud cry escapes.

'Don't beat up the bloody child!' the man with the long beard shouts at her, getting up to his feet and using hand gestures.

'He won't listen to me!' says the woman.

'It's because you did not train him well. It's your fault,' says the other man. 'What's wrong with you women? You don't know how to rear up children anymore.'

This does not sit well with Omega.

She springs to the woman's defence. 'And what's wrong with you men?' she asks. 'Do you even have children of your own for you to lecture her? Let her be. Heh women this, women that, nonsense! If she didn't train him up well, then where was the father of the child, heh? Tell me. Where was the father?'

Omega is up on her seat, lashing out until there is dead silence in the bus and the woman is back on her seat, smiling. The boy is in a flood of tears, but much more composed, as she holds him in her arms. In a few minutes, he is asleep. The woman looks back at Omega and mouths the words 'thank you' without expressing it audibly. Omega gives her a thumps up and the rest of the journey is much more peaceful.

They drop off the bus in the CBD, at around 1030am, and catch a *kombi* to Warren Park. The church service has already begun, so they hurry. Harare seems much more organised and clean to Mercy, despite the hordes of *kombis* causing havoc on the roads and the swarm of vendors who are on the streets, even on a Sunday morning.

In the suburb, they are directed to the church which is on the edge of the hill. It is a sprawling building, larger than Fire Rain, with several halls that are almost full when they arrive. They are welcomed at the gate by two girls dressed in purple and white, who lead them to the chairs in the back of the main auditorium. Hordes of people are streaming in, and on the platform in the front, on the left side of the altar, a fully-robed choir is singing, backed by a complete band.

Mercy scans the room for Munamato, finding him lying prostrate on the carpeted floor close to the choir, in a picture of total surrender. If the atmosphere in Sakubva is glorious, then this has to be heaven itself. Even Omega feels a tugging at her heart. She needs to consider religion seriously, she thinks.

The singing over, they all sit down.

Munamato is up on his feet and one of the boys is wiping the dust off his shiny black suit. He sits down, on a huge white chair that is like a throne, next to an equally dressed beautiful woman with a baby in her arms. In a few minutes, he is up on the pulpit, accompanied by a deafening round of applause and shouts of 'Amen', to do what he knows best. He is still ignorant of Mercy's presence in the house.

'My wife and I are grateful for all your labour of love,' he says. 'There is no way that we could have made it this far without your faithfulness and support. God will reward you richly, in this age and in that which is to come…'

Mercy wants to stand up and wave at him, but Omega pulls her down, back to the seat, grabbing her by the arm so she does not embarrass them both.

Meanwhile, Munamato announces an upcoming wedding for a young couple. He asks them to come up to the front. There will also be a conference in two months' time, which will be held in Domboshava.

The message which he delivers, after a reading of the scriptures, invokes a mighty response from the congregants. They jump out of their seats and hysterically shout, 'Amen'. As he continues to reference her in his preaching, it becomes clearer to Mercy and Omega, that the woman sitting in front is his wife, that Omega was right when she said the man could have moved on. There is turmoil inside Mercy, much like someone is stirring seething *sadza* right inside her head. She is boiling, certainly not caught up in the glorious atmosphere they are all swimming in. Omega is busy keeping her calm, assuring her that they will deal with this after the service.

The service over, people start streaming out of the building. Mercy literally sprints to the front, to confront Munamato, Omega right on her tail. Munamato sees her from afar and is up on his feet as if he is about to run away, but with his wife's hand firmly placed in his and her other holding the bouncing baby boy who is also dressed in a suit and bow tie, he can't escape in a hurry.

'Hey sister, where are you going?' one of the boys, a bouncer, asks, blocking her way. 'You can't see the pastor now as he is tired. You will have to book an appointment…'

He is standing in the way with his arms outstretched, but Mercy is not having any of it. She ducks under the huge arms and brushes past him. 'Munamato! Munamato!' she calls, and Munamato's wife turns her head. 'Munamato, are you sure you can do this to me, heh? So this is the reason why you have not returned my calls, heh?'

The bouncer tries again to drag her from behind. He scratches her butt instead, to which she turns around and slaps him right in the face.

'Let her come through,' says Munamato.

Mercy presents herself before his face, seething with anger.

'Who is she?' asks Munamato's wife. Unsettled.

'She is Mercy. The girl I told you about.'

'What does she want?'

He doesn't answer the question, but asks Mercy and Omega to come through to his office, which is just next to the altar, so they can discuss their issue in private. His wife and the bouncer follow behind them.

'Don't worry about this, honey, I will handle it,' he assures his wife, but still she follows behind, the baby in her arms. She sits next to him in the huge office as the bouncer closes the door and waits outside.

Mercy is still fuming.

'What can I do for you, Sister Mercy?' Munamato asks.

His words like a sword driven through her chest, she feels the blood gushing out of her wounded heart. She doesn't say a word.

'Pastor. I guess this is your wife?' asks Omega.

'Right, my sister, this is my wife,' he replies, calm as a cucumber. He seems to have waited for this day. He is certainly prepared for it.

'I see,' continues Omega. 'I guess that she already knows that you duped my sister? That you promised to marry her, you slept with her and promised to come back to Sakubva for her. But, now you have the temerity to open your loud stinking mouth to say, 'What can I do for you Sister Mercy.' What kind of a pastor are you?'

'Is this true?' asks the wife, looking at Munamato. 'Please tell me this is not what happened?'

'Listen, honey, I will explain,' he says. 'Mercy and I have a history, that's all. I never promised to marry her.'

'Liar! Liar,' shouts Mercy. She had thought that she would kill him if she found out that he deceived her, but now she feels powerless, like all her strength has been sucked out by a goblin from Chipinge. 'Why did you do that to me? Why? Why are you doing this Munamato?'

'Listen, Mercy,' he says. 'It is over between you and me. I was a boy and you were a girl. Period. I don't know all else you are talking about or where you are getting it from. I have my wife and I am enjoying life. Yes, you were my girlfriend. Yes, I loved you, then. But look, I decided to settle with my wife and I am happily married. I suggest that you keep yourself well and find a God-fearing husband to start your own family with. Perhaps you should go find the father of your child and ask him to marry you...'

Omega shakes her head in disgust. 'Pastor!' she says as she claps her hands, disappointed. 'You call yourself pastor, heh? May your God have mercy on you? Let's go my sister.'

She grabs Mercy by the arm and storms out of the office, dragging her along since she has neither the strength nor the will to move. She feels like she should just die, like there is nothing else to live for.

The journey back to Mutare is long. They feel every inch of it. Mercy is quietly crying, albeit with no more tears coming out of her. Omega assures her that what happened to her is common, that she is not the first or the last one to suffer such, that even she was disappointed in her life, not only once or even twice.

Many times.

'You see, little sister,' Omega says. 'You see a good girl like me, like your aunty that you talk about, you see us like this, past our prime and not married, and people think that we were stupid, that we prostituted ourselves with the boys and that's why we are not married. But the truth, *munin'inc*, is that for each of us that you see there is more than double the number of men who shattered our hearts. Who played us like footballs. It's life, and we just have to live with it. Those who have been lucky to settle down, some of them think that they were clever, that they deserved it. But what can we say? We don't have the credentials to even question them. So, take heart little sister, this is not the end of the world. Welcome to life. As for me, well, I am done with men. If anything, I seek only to use them just like they have used me all these years.'

These lectures do nothing to reassure Mercy. They push her further to the brink.

When they arrive in Sakubva it is now dark. Omega offers Mercy to sleep at her rented one room, but she refuses. She walks her home, to MaNcube's place, which is just down the road.

They are on the curve, a few metres to the house, when they see Pastor Jonathan's car parked outside, and a few people milling around the street. Mercy's heart skips like a kid of goat when they are closer and can clearly hear the singing in the yard.

Tinashe, being one of the people by the road, meets them halfway. 'She is gone,' he says in a sorrowful voice.

Mercy is stunned. She feels dizzy, like she felt the day she fainted after VaMusungwa beat her with the fan belt. She slumps onto the dust in the middle of the road. Her crying is not audible, but one can feel the deep cracks in her heart as she is thrust back into the deep like the bible's Job.

Fifteen

Sleeping demons

She wouldn't be here if it was someone else's funeral. The last people she wants to be around are those from the church. She doesn't even want to be near Reverend Mbudzi or Tinashe or, worse still, Mother. They are all wolves in sheep's clothing. None of them is godly and besides, if their God truly exists, why did he allow all these things to happen to her? Why did he fold his arms and allow people to trample all over her like this? She hates him, has deep resentment for their God. It spreads through her soul like a virus, her heart is consumed by an overwhelming desire for revenge.

MaNcube's body is lowered into the ground on the edge of the hill, wrapped up in a brand-new blanket bought by

Tinashe, her rugged bible placed on top. Then, heap after heap of the red soil is loaded on top of her until it is a small mound. It is difficult for Mercy. She feels like she is the one wrapped up in the blanket. She can sense the weight of the soil being poured on top of her.

It is yet another turning point for her, and she has no clue which way she will go. MaNcube was now like a mother to her, someone she could share her troubles with and not be judged. But now here she is, buried next to her Mundewere and mourned by strangers, buried in a blanket instead of a casket as no one could buy her one. If life has been tough for Mercy, she knows that it has been tougher for MaNcube.

She cannot help thinking that this, what is happening now, could easily happen to her in the future, unless things change, somehow. The thought of it makes her shiver. She kneels on the side of the grave and takes the sand into her hands, as the mourners make their way back to their homes. Feeling the sand and the small stones sinking into her bare knees, she weeps.

Tinashe squats next to her and rests his hand on her left shoulder in a reassuring manner. When everyone is gone back to their homes to eat *sadza* with their families and to forget about MaNcube for the rest of their lives, Tinashe walks her to the empty house left by her adopted mother, to a house of loneliness and sorrow. In the end, just like the others, he also leaves for his own house.

She is in denial for many days, until it gradually sinks into her, what her life has become. With MaNcube gone and her hope of settling down with Munamato up in flames, she finds herself in a dark place, a place of hopelessness and despair. She is angry. She looks behind and sees her life engulfed in darkness. She projects forward and all she can see is darkness and gloom. It changes her. It awakens the sleeping demons that, for what now seems like a fleeting moment, laid low at the bottom of her soul. She embraces it, the darkness, considers herself a fool for having in the first place believed that a man with a pendulum swinging between his legs just like Father, could be different, for having thought that something better could come out of her life. If Munamato, a pastor, was capable of doing that to her, then what hope does anyone else have? Who can be trusted? It is a lie, she concludes, that anybody cares for anybody. It is dog eat dog in this life, and she is done being the one who gets to be eaten all the time, one who gets to be swallowed with their eyes wide open like *kapenta* fish from Kariba dam. If he could do that to her and it is accepted as the order of life, then no one should judge whatever she does.

So, like this, she finds herself more and more in the company of Omega and less and less in the company of the church-people. Eventually, she moves in with her, into her one room up the road. She follows her to the *shebeens* and beerhalls during the night, at first just for a distraction, and eventually for play. Her eyes have now opened. The only way to survive in this battered country, despite the virus that has prematurely sent many youths to the ground and which now scares her not, is to use the men just as they have used her. 'It's a win-win,' Omega says.

Little by little, she finds herself being sucked into the mire, legs first, before her whole body plunges into the vast waters of the sinkhole and is swept downstream with virtually no resistance.

Tonight is her first encounter, and it is with a huge bearded man who stinks of alcohol and of lack of soap and water, who does not use protection and vomits twice before the act. She closes her nostrils with a wet towel which she finds on the pillow, but she finds that it stinks of urine as if the man urinates or *wanks* on it. She tosses it back to the floor.

The man's room, at the timber factory, only has a single bed in one corner, with old blankets and plates strewn all over the place, a few of the plates finding their way to under the bed. The paraffin stove in the other corner is hardly used, and the old *sadza* that is covered in a plastic plate on top of the stove is now moulding.

Moments ago, when they came to the house, he drove her in the horse of the company's huge *gonyeti* truck which he parked just outside, next to another that is in the same yard. She expected to see a house much better than this, but being a novice she agreed to get dirty with him before he paid anything.

He is on top of her, heaving and breathing high like Father when he raped her a few years ago. The smell of the alcohol makes this like *déjà vu*. Tensing her brain, she shuts herself out of any feeling. She has not at this time learnt how to do the fake sounds, as she will surely learn in the future, so she is very much like a dead person or plastic doll. The man doesn't care, anyway, as his first lasts about a minute and a half. He dozes off at the beginning of the second. She is glad.

If she could see tomorrow, right now she could be ransacking the house for something to grab as compensation for dealing with this. She could be emptying his pockets or taking the watch. But no, she is a novice. She sleeps next to him, and when he wakes up in the early hours of the morning he is onto her one more time, this time wide awake.

She is proud of having survived the ordeal. She feels that she has been initiated and earned the right to be a really bad girl. Happily, she demands her compensation.

'What money?' asks her host, with a screwed face.

'For my services, of course.'

'What services? Are you a prostitute?'

'No. I am not … I want my money. You knew …'

She is not comfortable enough to say it. Prostitute. The sound of it scares her, but the reality of it is that she did this for the money, in order to survive. In one way, she is just trying to survive in a world that has no love, but in the actual fact she is it. A prostitute.

'If you are not a prostitute, then there is no money for you,' says the man, buckling his trousers. 'We are two grown up persons that enjoyed the night together, so why should I pay you?'

'It's not fair. You know you should pay. It's not fair.'

'Get out of my house! Bloody prostitute! I have to go to work and I don't have time for this nonsense.'

'But this is not fair, you know it's not fair.'

'I am not your mother,' he says, emptying the back pocket of his pants of a few bearer cheques not enough for a *kombi* ride. 'Use this for transport,' he says.

He leaves the house unlocked and Mercy sitting on the little mattress, drowning in her sorrows. She gathers herself together, wipes off a tear or two, and grabs the few notes from the side of the paraffin stove. She looks around to see if there is anything else she can grab. None of it is good enough. She will have to sort it out with Mati, Omega's friend who hooked her up with this man. Unbeknown to her, Mati and Omega were already paid by the man last night to hook him up with her.

When she leaves the room, the man is already driving away, the darkness is quickly dispersing, and the sun is almost emerging from its hiding place underneath the earth. She hurries off and away from the compound, bumping into some of the women who are busy sweeping their sandy yards with hard brooms made from wild shrubs, who look at her disapprovingly, scrutinising her colourful short dress and high heels which are making it hard for her to walk in the sand. She ignores them and hits the tarred road back to Sakubva.

She doesn't use the money as that is all that is between her and an empty tummy In any case, it is not enough to take her to her destination. She walks, telling herself that walking is justified as there are not many *kombis* operating at this time, that she would have to wait for a long time to catch one. On the way, she re-evaluates her resolve. She decides that it is better for her to be Mapudege than Mother. Life has handed her lemons, so she might as well make some lemonade. It is time for breaking bad, to eat the whole dog and its puppy.

Now a pro, her hunting grounds no longer include only men drunk from alcohol, but also those who are drunk of the spirit. After all, the people who really hurt her are the church-people. They owe her lots, and she will make them pay.

After a long time, she is back at Faire Rain on Sundays, this time with a different agenda. Many of the church-people are aware of what happened between her and Munamato, but none of them has a clue what she has become as a result. All they see is a beautiful girl struggling with life, no different than any other in the country. Her suitors, the ones she rejected in the past, are happy to see her again. For them, it is another opportunity to try their luck, like *manna* from heaven.

Omega does not understand Mercy's obsession with the church. 'Listen *munin'ina*,' she says, 'none of these people are Munamato, you understand? If you really are to revenge in that way, then you should go deal with him in Harare, directly. After all, he is a man, if you pursue him enough he might even cheat on his wife with you.'

Mercy is adamant. 'None of these people are innocent,' she says. 'There is no difference. Munamato and them, same *fanana.*'

'I don't think it's a good idea, *munin'ina.* I just thought I should let you know. Be smart about it. Who knows, if our deal with the Moza guys works out, we could even be out of this business, completely. It is not all about revenge, but survival. Then we can enjoy life, properly ...'

Mercy simply laughs this off and does not change her plans. She keeps going after the church, deliberately booking dubious appointments with each of Pastor Jonathan's young pastors, seducing them with the smooth talk she has now mastered.

First to fall is a young trainee pastor from Kadoma, called Wisdom, who because of his zeal chases after her from the word go, following up on her and quizzing her for missing most of the church meetings. Slowly, she leads him into the dungeon, flirting with his busy eyes until they are popping, flashing her flesh indiscreetly until his mind is a hive of fleshly imaginations, slowly winding the rope around his neck until all that is required is a little spark.

Wisdom convinces himself that he is just doing the Lord's work. He refuses to accept that he is dining with the devil, until when his tummy is full, when he is caught up in a way that would require a great mission to placate him from her clutch, to deliver him from the command of his fleshly desire.

'Sister Mercy,' he says when they are in Omega's room, on her bed. 'We should not be doing this. This is all wrong. Maybe we should get married, you know, so we can be saved from this sin?'

Mercy laughs at him, enjoying herself: 'Marry me you say, pastor? Why? Because you are feeling guilty?'

'Of course, Sister Mercy. What we are doing is wrong ...'

'So, stop it then ...'

'I can't,' he says, helplessly, and sighs.

She suggests that the best way for him would be to confess his sin in front of the whole church. That would embarrass him enough to make it an effective deterrent for his sneaking into her room every Sunday night after church. Wisdom does consider the suggestion. At first, he agrees that he will do it, that it would be better for him to lose one eye and enter into heaven than keep both and end up in hell, but after Mercy teases him and dares him to make the announcement during the Easter conference, he decides against the idea, realising that it would kill his career. She rubs it into him until after a few months of winning and losing in controlling his passions, of being at one time a holy Man of God and at other times a brilliant fornicator, he asks for a transfer back to Kadoma. In a few months, he marries one lucky girl there.

Mercy is happy for him because, after all, he is a good man. But, because of this, she does not feel that she has been adequately appeased of the great harm inflicted on her by one of his kind. So, she decides that she will finish them all, one after the other, until she has proven that none of them is going to heaven, that life is all about the strong abusing the weak. This time around she will be the abuser.

Next in line is a married pastor who replaces Pastor Jonathan as the senior pastor at Fire Rain, Pastor Jonathan having been transferred to another branch elsewhere in the country.

The name of the newbie is Pastor Goodness. He is a bit of a problem at first, rightly pointing out Mercy's pretentions of being possessed by an evil spirit during prayer. He seems to be more experienced than the others. When he invites Mercy for counselling, he always has his pastor wife, Gloria, by his side. He and Gloria try to bring her closer, to make her their adopted child. Gloria feels that she could be a sister to her. She tries to understand where she is coming from and where she is going.

'Sister Mercy,' Gloria says one day, 'you should be more serious about your faith. Why do you not attend our youth meetings? You see, my sister, you deserve a good husband to settle down with and to make a family, and it is in these meetings that we teach these kinds of things.'

Because of her passion gap, Gloria is very beautiful when she smiles, and Mercy can see the determination in her eyes and the genuineness of her kindness. She feels pity for her. Who does she think she is? After all, she was just lucky to marry, she is no more special than MaNcube or Tete or Omega or her.

'I will come, pastor,' she says. 'It's only that I will be working some of the time. As you can see, things are not easy in this country.'

'I know. Let me know if I can be of any help.'

'Thank you, pastor.'

'What do you do anyway, your job?'

'Various things, whatever is giving money at the time.'

'Just be careful. You are too beautiful to waste, and as a child of God, you should not get yourself involved in shady deals.'

The elders say that the dog that you feed with fat milk is the one that will bite you tomorrow. Gloria is well aware of this, but she suspects nothing of that sort from her new friend. Her bigger mistake, however, is that she invites her into her home. She is there before and after church, and during weekends.

Omega is concerned. 'Please don't wreck that marriage, Mercy,' she says. 'That woman loves you and you don't find people like that anymore.'

Mercy laughs it off and goes after her prize with great determination. The good pastor is caught off guard, after he becomes less guarded due to their increasing closeness, allowing her to come into his office when he is alone.

He walks into the trap.

It is a Saturday. He is alone at the church office as Gloria is attending a women's conference in Chiredzi. Mercy comes in as usual, this time bearing goods. Things happen so fast that Pastor Goodness only comes back to his good senses after he has already crossed the line, right there, on the carpet of his office which is located just behind the church altar.

It eats at him for a number of months. But, he does it again. And again. Every time, after she is gone and he thinks about his wife and the vows which he made, he cries, but when he meets her again he finds himself doing the same thing as if he is on autopilot, as if he is possessed by the devil himself.

The one person who seems too much for Mercy to mess up with is Tinashe. He still comes after her at various times, innocently and unaware of the happenings behind the scenes. Every time after he is gone, she cries after him. He is too innocent and straightforward. He exposes her wickedness.

'It doesn't matter that the pastor dumped you,' he says. 'I still love you, Mercy, and I think you should give me a chance.'

'Tinashe, you really don't know me. I am a bad girl. Bader than you can imagine.'

'I don't care about that,' he says with his head tilted to one side. 'I love you. I know it will work between us.'

'I am not ready Tinashe, I don't think I will ever be ...'

'I will be patient with you. I will wait for you to heal.'

And wait he waits. He has no idea of Mercy's involvement with Pastor Goodness or of her nightly dealings with Omega and Mati. All he sees is an angel sent from heaven, for which it would be a privilege to share in her glory. All he wants is to make her happy, to rescue her from the shame of having been dumped by a pastor. She knows he means it, but she is too deep to drag him into her mess. In as far as she is concerned, she would be happy to see him happily married to a good woman, perhaps to someone like Chipo, not her.

Sixteen

Mati's *ganja*

Neither Pastor Goodness's infidelity nor his sinking low and deep into it surprises her. She has come to expect that of all men. When he becomes craftier in cheating his wife, taking Mercy to different lodges in as far places as Harare and Kariba, it becomes clearer to her what Mother used to say, that men are dogs. She would add, however, that they are a whole dog and a pig put together, not half and half. What surprises her though, is the blindness with which Gloria continues to revere and deify her husband like he is a saint, even after Mercy shows up at their house several times in his car, scantily dressed after having romped with him at the church office. Still Gloria doesn't suspect a thing. Even when Mercy sleeps at their house because she and Gloria are to go to the town of Rusape for a meeting in the morning, and Pastor Goodness sneaks out of the bed that he shares with Gloria in the middle of the night and finds himself in Mercy's embrace like a baby, even so, Gloria is so clouded that she doesn't notice anything. She wakes up in the morning to prepare for the trip, and doesn't at all notice that her husband is still sleeping next door. He only sneaks back in when she is bathing, and when she comes back to the room he is snoring. She kisses him on the mouth, happily, as she and Mercy leave the house a few minutes later.

It is not easy for Pastor Goodness, for he actually does love his wife and, when he is in his right mind, regrets having got himself caught up in this affair. So, when he snaps back from the life of death that he has lived all along and remembers his calling, after gathering a lot of strength through prayer and having set it aside for many weeks, he decides to tell Mercy that he wants out.

'Eh, Mercy,' he says with a little cough, '... Sister Mercy. Eh, I think we should stop this affair. You see, my wife told me that she is pregnant with our first child. I can't mess around anymore.'

'So, what are you saying, Goodness? That you are dumping me?'

'No, no, Mercy ... eh, Sister Mercy, what I am saying is that, it is time to stop.'

'Why?'

'Because this was not meant to last. You knew that I was married.'

'It was not meant to last, huh. So what was it meant to do?'

'C'mon, sweetheart, you know what I mean. See, you are still my beauty. You can find a fine young man to marry in the church. I can even arrange it for you if you like. That Tinashe boy, for instance, he seems to be so much into you. I don't want to jeopardise your chances of getting married. You are so beautiful, to the point of causing a Man of God like me to forget his vows. Please, Mercy.'

It makes sense, what he is saying, but she is not foolish enough to not see that his reasons are self-serving. He has had enough of her, so she does not mean much to him anymore. She doesn't care anyway, about this not being loved, because she doesn't believe it after all. But she won't let this end on his terms as if he is the one who started it.

'No,' she says. 'This is not over.'

'What do you mean?'

'I mean; you can't dump me like this.'

'Why?'

'Because I am also pregnant for you.'

He feels like he is about to faint. His mind explodes into different pieces. 'That is impossible Mercy, I know you are on the pill,' he says.

'Which is 100% effective?'

'Stop it. You know I can't marry you. Even if you were to be pregnant, you know the right thing would be to get rid of it. How would you face Gloria?'

That is it. That is all she wanted for her to be 100 percent that all he is after is to cover his own backside, not hers. The mention of abortion brings back terrible memories to her. She doesn't tell him, but she will destroy him, completely. His attitude perfectly fits the bill for her revenge, for the evil Munamato meted out to her. She does not tell him that the pregnancy is a lie, just as he too doesn't tell her that he was lying about Gloria's pregnancy. She 'agrees' to remove the 'pregnancy,' but only with his help.

'I knw of a lady in Honde Valley,' she says to him in a text message the following day.

'Brilliant!' he replies.

'Will u cum with mi since you r the fthr?'

'No way. You know I am a pstr'

'So wht? When you cried btwn my legs had you frgtten tht u ar one?'

'Don't say tht pliz. U knw my wife cld c thse msgs one day'

'Am nt afraid of her. Shez a woman jst lk mi'

'Pliz I beg. Dnt do ths'

'Will u cum w mi?'

'Yes darling bt pliz delete the msgs nhaika?'

'Will do. Gud nyt and sleep tyt'

The texting continues, on his side religiously deleting these as soon as he reads them, and every time that they meet reemphasising the need to have these deleted from her phone too. She doesn't.

Soon, it will be time to put her plan into motion. She will do it at the mid-week meeting at Fire Rain, where Bishop Ndoro has travelled all the way from Harare for a week-long revival meeting. He is preaching on Wednesday night, on love and fellowship.

She will be early.

Wednesday comes, and she is faithful to her promise. Pastor Goodness and Gloria are in the church with the other pastors, and so is Munamato, who travelled with Bishop Ndoro. His wife is with him and is pregnant with their second child. When Mercy sees them, her brain swells up and fills her skull. A brewing begins to take shape inside of her, stirring like a whirlwind dancing on the dusty fields of Murewa.

She composes herself as she walks all the way to sit in the front, close to the pastors.

When Munamato sees her, he becomes tense on the inside, but feigns calmness. He waves at her from his cushioned seat. The other congregants who are well aware of their previous relationship, like Tinashe, are curious. They stretch their heads like giraffes to try and pick up clues from the faceoff.

There is an altar call at the end of the preaching.

Many people stream to the front to be prayed for. Bishop Ndoro invites Munamato, Pastor Goodness, Gloria and the other two pastors present, to pray for them. Mercy is infuriated and disgusted by the whole picture of Munamato and Pastor Goodness laying their hands on the faithful and declaring them healed, standing side by side as if they are the bible's John and James. She isn't healed from Munamato's having trampled on her heart, and she isn't healed of the abuse that she suffered at the hands of pimps and pastors like Pastor Goodness. She feels that it is not fair for these two to stand there declaring in foreign tongues and religious proclamations that the people are healed, quoting the holy scriptures which she still doesn't understand, when they themselves are so full of s**t. So, when this finishes and it is time for testimonies, she is the first one to stand up and run to the microphone. Munamato smiles at her, thinking that she has probably healed from the heartbreak that he inflicted on her.

'Firstly, I want to thank God that I am alive today,' she begins. 'I know that you all believe in God, genuinely, and that you are truly blessed when the Men of God pray for you. But it is not so for some of us who have been abused by these pastors. You see, when you sleep with someone who is not a pastor, who is not your husband, you can live with it. You can come to church and ask for forgiveness, and feel forgiven. But when it is the pastor who goes after you demanding sex, it is such a disgrace ...'

Bishop Ndoro and Brother Mike, who are leading the proceedings, are shocked by this. The congregation is all gasps as people try to understand what is taking place. Brother Mike tries to grab the microphone away from her before they are further embarrassed. 'Thank you, sister, thank you.'

She doesn't let go, but screams into it for all to hear: 'They all slept with me, these pastors of yours, ... Munamato ... Goodness ...'

She is like a tornado by the time she is whisked away into Pastor Goodness's office by one of the elders and the service is cut short.

Bishop Ndoro tries to reassure the congregants that he will look into the issue, and to urge them not to come to hasty conclusions. The remaining meetings are postponed to the weekend. He rounds up the male pastors to talk to them in Pastor Goodness's office, but Gloria refuses to be left out since she is also a pastor, so he decides to proceed with the meeting with her being present.

Mercy is seated quietly in one of the chairs, as well as the other pastors, except for Bishop Ndoro who is pacing around the room and shaking his head.

'I want to deal with this once and for all,' he says, fuming. 'I have never been humiliated like this in my whole life as a minister, so I will not beat about the bush. The sister is here, so I need somebody to please tell me exactly what is happening? Have we stooped this low?'

'This girl, bishop, she doesn't know what she is talking about,' Munamato is first off the mark. 'All that she has against me, you all know, is that I didn't marry her. That's all. Nothing more. She is possessed by a demon ... and this is exactly why I refused to marry her ...'

'Yes, this can only be demonic,' says Pastor Goodness. 'How can someone grab a mic like that in front of the whole church? Bishop, we must avoid trying to reason with a demon. She needs really good counselling, this girl. Clearly, the devil is operating through her ...'

Mercy does not say a word, but maintains a calm gaze.

'Nonsense!' slams Bishop Ndoro. 'I do not see any demon here. Are you demon-possessed, you, are you?'

Mercy shakes her head. She is not crying.

'Mercy,' Gloria says, 'is this true?'

'Yes, it is.'

'What evidence is there for all this?' asks Pastor Goodness. 'Why should we just believe this nonsense for which there is absolutely no evidence?'

'Yes, where is the evidence?' asks Munamato.

'Gentlemen,' Bishop Ndoro intervenes, 'I will handle this my way, so you shut up. Mercy; that is your name isn't it? What happened, and when? I want the facts here because this your charge against my pastors is a strong one.'

'Ask them,' she says, 'they know it.'

'Liar! Liar!' shouts Munamato.

'Bishop, I respect you just like I respected Pastor Jonathan,' she says. 'But these your pastors, sir, I am sorry, because none of them is clean. What you should be asking them is how many times they slept with me in this office, each of them, not whether or not they did. How many times did they sneak into my house and how many lodges did they book for us?'

'Liar! Liar,' Munamato fumes, jumping out of his chair. Bishop Ndoro orders him to sit down. 'It's not her who is talking bishop. It's a demon, I am telling you,' he continues.

'Yes, bishop, this can't be true,' Pastor Goodness adds.

Mercy laughs, sarcastically, so hard that there is immediate silence in the room: 'Did you not sleep with me, Goodness, in the spare bedroom in your house when your wife was sleeping just next door, that time I went to Rusape with her? Do you deny it?'

'What?' Gloria jumps to her feet. '. . . But he was with me all night?'

Mercy laughs again. 'Then, what is this?' she says as she pulls out her phone with the undeleted text messages between her and Pastor Goodness. 'Is this not your husband's number?'

Gloria grabs the phone from her and when she reads the messages, crumbles to the ground. Pastor Goodness and Munamato storm out of the meeting, protesting that Bishop Ndoro is entertaining a demon instead of listening to them. When he goes through the messages himself, Bishop Ndoro is hugely disappointed. There is no doubt in his mind that his compatriots have indeed done the unthinkable.

When Gloria wakes up, she is like a zombie.

Mercy looks at her with pity. 'I am sorry, Gloria,' she says before she too storms out of the room, leaving Bishop Ndoro to spend hours trying to counsel Gloria, achieving very little in the process. She does not stop crying. Neither does she go back to her house.

When Mercy arrives at Mati's house in the night, she finds Omega and the girls in the company of two men; one Zimbabwean and the other, Almando, a Mozambique national. It is in the middle of the night and there is no *shebeen* tonight at Mati's three-bedroom house. There is only the nine of them in the house, which is full of *ganja*-infested smoke and brown alcohol bottles. In the corner, close to the kitchen, are boxes upon boxes, previously used for carrying oranges, stacked up to the roof and full of the 'weed', destined for Mozambique.

'So, this is how it will work,' Almando says in a funny Shona accent, typical of people from the Mozambique province of Manica, 'we call the driver and he comes over with a few of the other boxes with the oranges, we load these in between, then he goes back to the depot to load the rest of the oranges on top. So, we sandwich the product.'

'Machipanda is not easy,' says Mati. 'It is easy, I think, to be suspected at the border post as most trucks go through Nyamapanda. If we decide to go through Nyamapanda, we would firstly have to go back all the way to Macheke, which increases the risk of us getting caught.'

'True,' says Almando. 'Which is why we will go through Mt Selinda, into Espungabera. I know all the people on the route.'

Although she took no part in sourcing the product, Mercy's role in the deal is not without risk. She has to accompany the driver, together with Almando and the other Zimbabwean man, all the way to Beira. Her good looks and smooth talk will be an effective distraction to police officers and border control.

'I'm done with the church,' Mercy announces to the group.

'What did you do Mercy?' asks Omega, curiously.

'Nothing, but it is now over. No more.'

Omega grills her until she spits out the truth. She is sad for Gloria, but happy that Mercy now has settled her score with the church-people. Now she can move forward and be more independent. That Munamato was among those humiliated adds to her pleasure. She also thinks that Mercy was very brave to have done that. She has now toughened to life and that is good for her. 'Well done, *munin'ina*,' she says.

Mercy hits the road with Almando and the other man. On the way, they decide to change the plan and to enter Mozambique through an informal opening in rural Chipinge, that is often used for smuggling cotton and other goods by the villagers using ox-drawn scotch carts. The villagers refuse to recognise the border which was imposed on them by their colonisers years ago, cutting tribes and clans into half. In as far as they are concerned, the people of Mozambique's Manica and Tete provinces are kinsmen to those of Zimbabwe's Manicaland, and in the south where they cross into Mozambique, the people speak the same Ndau dialect as their Zimbabwean counterparts. In fact, Almando's other uncles live on the Zimbabwean side of the border. To them, the border does not exist.

Since it is in the night, they turn off the lights of the UD vehicle and use the moonlight. There are no mishaps until they are deep into Mozambique, when they are locked up in a rural police station for the night. They pay the required bribe, in US dollars, to the several policemen, who are then happy to let them go. The rest of the journey is without incident, apart from the uneven, bumpy dusty roads that they negotiate all the way until they are on the narrow, tarred road.

Mercy and the men are stuck in Beira for many days, until the product ships and they exchange the money bags with the other gang. It is not all sorrowful there. Since it is New Year, they get to party in the streets with the jubilant Mozambique nationals who fill up every corner with live bands on New Year's Eve, like in a carnival. Mercy makes the most of it, using it to effectively forget her issues with the Fire Rain people, dancing to Oliver

Mutukudzi's songs which she, strangely, finds every band playing in Mozambique. It is just like she is back home, except that the people here are much happier.

The trouble comes after they count the money and realise that they got only a small fraction of what was agreed upon. The other gang has already disappeared. Having no other option, they spend the next day travelling in a *kombi* all the way back to Mutare, without Almando or the driver, unsure how they are going to explain this to their friends.

Seventeen

The shrine

S he doesn't go back to Fire Rain and no-one follows after her, except for Tinashe who, despite her unwillingness to talk to him, continues texting and leaving voicemails on her mobile phone as if he is possessed by a spirit.

Munamato and Pastor Goodness are kicked out of the church, and they relocate to the town of Gweru where they plant a church of their own. Meanwhile, many of the Fire Rain congregants join other churches or simply stop churching altogether, even after Bishop Ndoro brings back Pastor Jonathan to try and stabilise the sinking ship. Some of them continue to wander around like lost sheep, trying to make sense of the meaning of their faith, if after all it means anything to anyone. Mercy doesn't care. She doesn't feel anything at all, not even for Gloria, who having divorced her husband quits the church and now runs an orphanage in Mutoko, looking after children whose parents died from the HIV AIDS pandemic.

Mati's *ganja* didn't pay much in the end, although for a while it gave her and the gang enough to have a sort of reprieve from the hard work. They plan on doing bigger deals in the future, and on making this their source of livelihood. Mercy is now much closer to them, sinking deeper into their ways. When she hears of Tete's illness from her friends in the CBD, she resists doing anything about it until after many days. Then, she decides to visit her at the house.

She finds her bedridden, and the sight of her brings back memories of MaNcube, but she doesn't cry. She doesn't know whether she can genuinely cry anymore.

'Mercy, my niece,' Tete says in a dying voice, 'I am glad that you have come to visit me. I did not treat you well the last time. Please forgive me ... I am truly sorry.'

Sorry, Mercy thinks. She should be sorry for herself and not for her. She is the one who lost a boyfriend and has now lost her health. 'Forget about it, aunty,' she says, 'that was many years ago, and I was only a child. How are you feeling now?'

'Not well my niece. Not at all. The doctors can't see anything wrong with me, so they discharged me from the hospital. At least they did not mention the virus, which is some good news. That is what scares me, Mercy, the virus. I just pray that I do not have it in my blood.'

'It will be well, aunty,' she says, before changing the subject. 'How is Tribulation?' she asks. 'Have you been to the village any recently?'

'Oh yes, I have been. Four months ago. It was just after I came back that this all started. He was doing well, and will be going to the mission school soon. Reverend Mbudzi organised it all for him. He still remembers the last time you visited with some man who had a car. My brother asks after that man every time I visit. Was it that pastor in the newspaper story the other day?'

'Aunty, I don't want to talk about it,' she says as she looks away. She pictures Munamato cuddling Tribulation and kissing him on the forehead at the village centre, leaning against the church truck. It doesn't hurt her anymore, but thinking about it still sets her on edge.

The reunion with Tete is not as difficult as she thought it would be, although she is still unwilling to come back to her house. Now, they both realise the folly of torturing themselves like they did for the past years instead of just burying the hatchet. It all now seems stupid that they fought over a man, a boy who never looked back after he was out of their lives. The last time Tete heard about Biggie was from those illegally sneaking into South Africa, running away from the debilitating economic conditions in the country. He is said to be leading a gang of *riff-raffs* smuggling people through the forests of Beitbridge, leaving them on the banks of the crocodile-infested Limpopo River to crawl into South Africa through the barbed wires. She doesn't care about him anymore. Neither does Mercy.

'When are you visiting him, Mercy?' Tete asks. 'When are you visiting your son?'

'I don't know. If Reverend Mbudzi is taking care of him, then that is all that matters to me. It's not like he will be excited to see me. I know that he hates me.'

'Don't say that my niece, he is still your blood.'

'I will see when I have the time.'

'Just try please, when you get a chance.'

'I will.'

'And Mercy,' Tete continues, 'I know you said that you don't know who his father is, but please I beg you in the name of God, if you know, you will have to tell him at some point. He will need to know his father. He is a boy, for goodness's sake.'

'I don't want to talk about that, aunty.'

Tete shakes her head, and they never talk about that again. Neither does Mercy ever go back to the village or come to live with Tete. Now she rents her own room in Sakubva, although she still hangs out with Omega and company. She is in and out of Tete's house and Omega comes with her a few of the times.

Tete's condition does not improve at all. She is now bedridden almost all the time, falling behind on her rent. The landlord, a poor old man and pensioner from Bocha, into whose bank account she deposits money every month for rent, is forced to come to the city to see for himself what the problem is. He has never had any problems with her before.

'I will get well and pay your money,' she begs him.

'But you are six months behind, and the rains are upon us. I need to buy seed and fertilizer for my crops. When will you be okay?'

'I don't know, *sekuru*, but I feel it in my bones. I will be okay soon.'

He is not convinced. He stays at the house for a couple more days, eating Tete's food and sleeping in the spare bedroom that used to be Mercy's room. At the end of his stay and before he leaves, he gives Tete an ultimatum. 'I am going back to the village to check on my cows,' he says, 'but if in two weeks' time my rent is still not paid, you will have to leave.'

Tete cries after he is gone. She has not felt as trapped and useless in her whole life, unable to use her hands to fend for herself like she has done since she was still a child growing up in the village. Now she will be forced to go back to the village, she thinks, but she does not have the strength or the money to transport her wasting self and the little possessions that she has. She does not have a room there either, so she will have to be accommodated by Father, perhaps in what used to be Mercy's hut, where she usually puts up when she visits them.

'If you go to the village, you will just die,' Mercy says when Tete informs her of her predicament. 'You should come live with me. At least I can look after you and take you to the hospital when I get some money. There are more options here in the city, including the herbs from the market.' Although she talks about the herbs, Mercy is quite aware that they did not keep MaNcube from dying despite her gobbling all the different varieties all day long.

'It won't make a difference my niece, whether I die or not. It is not as if I have children or a husband to live for.'

'Aunty please, ah. Don't talk like that.'

'It's the truth. And those herbs, they are not good. Who knows what they do to you? Who tested them anyway?'

'You think too much, aunty. How did our ancestors live before all this bottled medicine? Did they not live longer with our own traditional herbs?'

Tete does not have the strength to argue, and she has very little to say in the coming days when the landlord comes back and orders her out of the house. Mercy and Omega round up her few belongings and pack them into one of the rooms at Mati's. Then she moves in with Mercy in Sakubva. Now she is thin like a stick and her cheeks all fallen in. She has difficulty walking, so she walks slowly and drags her feet, and when Tinashe comes to the house one of the days, he offers to pray for her. Mercy does not like the idea, but because of her pity for Tinashe, she agrees.

'She will get better,' says Tinashe after the prayer, 'but you must come with her to the church when Bishop Ndoro visits.'

Tete agrees. Anything that gives her hope.

Mercy laughs it off. 'Forget it Tinashe,' she says. 'I will take my aunty to any church other than your Fire Rain circus. I will not do that.'

'I understand, Mercy. Whatever you say. But she needs prayers.'

Although she doesn't agree to go to the church, Mercy is aware of the problems she would have to deal with if Tete dies whilst she is living with her. She knows that Tete doesn't want to be buried in the city as if she is from Blantyre. But Mercy doesn't have the money to meet the smallest funeral expense. It scares her.

'I think your aunty could have been bewitched,' Omega says.

'You think so?'

'Of course, the fact that this is the city does not mean that there are no *varoyi*. All those her friends, like that one from Zaka, could have been jealous of her. She lived in that house by herself, didn't she? Surely, they would have been jealous of her.'

'So, what are you suggesting?'

'I don't know. I am just saying.'

'Should we take her to the church then, like Tinashe said?'

'Ummnn, that church? Maybe not. But I know of Madzibaba Babylon, who operates on the side of the road, towards Birchenough. He is really good.'

'You and *mapostori*. How do you know him, Omega?'

Omega laughs, then says, 'I am older than you, Mercy. I have been through a lot. You see, some time ago when clients were not forthcoming, when I was not being lucky, I visited him. He is clean, all he does is pray for you and give you these pebbles which you put in your bathing water every morning, the prayer tablets. They work.'

'Iii, my friend, I am not used to this *mapostori* thing. Does it work, really?'

She sits on it for a few days, until Tete starts talking funny like one who has lost their mind, then she panics. 'I will look after you my child,' Tete says to her. 'I know you have suffered enough, so I will tell them your story. I can see them now, I know that they love you.'

That settles it. She has to take her to Madzibaba Babylon's shrine. After all, he is not a witchdoctor, but one who consults with the spirit of God directly. He wears white garments, not black. If it could work for Tete, then why not give it a try?

Tinashe takes them to the shrine on a Friday afternoon, in his ex-Japanese hatchback which no longer shifts into gear number 3. He has to remember to skip that gear all the time. He does not quite agree with taking Tete to the shrine, but still he does it. For Mercy. Omega and Tete sit in the back, he and Mercy in the front. When they arrive at the open space that is the church, a vast expanse of land that Madzibaba Babylon grabbed for himself without seeking anyone's but the spirit's permission, there is a sea of white garments worn by the *mapostori*, who all have low haircuts and no make-up. Nobody dares question Madzibaba Babylon's land grabbing, for it is an open secret that because of the vast number of his following, he has a special place in the hearts of the rulers of the land. After all, it is his followers who are ferried by buses from across the country to receive the chief ruler at the airport, when he returns from his many errands in very far places.

Today, Mercy and Omega have also dispensed of their make-up. On their heads, they have tied these white cloths that are like hijabs, just like the many other women in the crowd. Tete is dressed the same way, but none of them has a white robe like most of the other people there.

They take off their shoes, just like the others, and leave them by the bushes close to the road, close to where Tinashe remains seated in the car after he refuses to go into the shrine with them. Mercy and Omega support Tete on their shoulders as they slowly walk the two-hundred-meter distance through the crowd, until they are close to the front. The men, big and small and many with long beards and bald heads, are sitting on one side in the dust, the women on the other, leaving a huge gap between them that is like a highway. In the highway, one bearded man is walking up and down, 'downloading' what the spirit is telling him and shouting at the top of his voice, declaring what he terms 'prophecies,' punctuated with choruses that the rest of the *mapostori* sing in amazing unison. They are up on their feet when the singing starts, bending their knees in a coordinated dance, clasping their hands together and bowing their heads, the men and the women facing each other. When the man in the highway stops, they sit down and listen to him channelling what the spirit is whispering only to him, rising up again when he resumes the singing or when one of the women suddenly bursts into song. They all seem to be committed.

The place does indeed feel like a holy ground.

Mercy looks around. Everyone seems to be so simple, although she notices quite quickly that none of them has a bible. They do not at all refer to the book. She doesn't believe in the bible, anyway, so she is really not bothered. At least, it is a departure from the Fire Rain kind of people. These simple, committed people, could be her salvation. She admires them.

After they have sat in the blazing sun for a good two hours, Madzibaba Babylon gets up to his feet from underneath the white garment where he lay all the time, and starts speaking. He too has a long beard although he seems young, much younger than many of the men and women in the gathering. He doesn't use the bible either, and there does not seem to be any organised programme. Omega explains that this is because they allow the spirit to lead instead of following human machinations.

Meanwhile, Tete is sleeping on Mercy's lap the whole time, and does not seem to care what's happening around her.

When the chanting is finished, Mercy and Tete join a long queue to the bushes where, behind a huge rock, Madzibaba Babylon is attending to the people, individually. He attends to those who have various issues and ailments, admonishing them to take the smooth pebbles which he says they should drop into their drinking and bath water. The pebbles are said to be so potent that even Australian border control would open their gates for you, even without a passport. No questions asked.

When it is their turn, Mercy and Tete go behind the rock. They find Madzibaba Babylon with his head covered in a white garment, except for the face, his long white robe which covers even his feet, tied in the waist with a red cloth belt. He is standing and looking at the ground as if avoiding their eyes, a bottle of water in his left hand and a heap of smooth pebbles on the ground, by his side. They kneel when they are close to him.

'I see a very dark cloud,' he says without even asking them why they are come. 'I see an old man's grave planted by an ant-hill. I see termites going in and out. I ask the angel Gabriel and he says to me, look my servant, the killers of men will pay with the lives of their children until their blood fills the rivers ...' At this, he pauses and shakes his head, and seems to question the angel is his vision. 'Why Gaburona, *raboni*? Michael. Rrrrrrrrhh!' He shakes his head again like a man who is troubled in his spirit. 'Rabby,' he continues, then addresses them. 'The problem, *Madzimai*, is not of your own making, and the vultures are circling. The spirit is saying that unless you commit your life to the church, there will be no change. But if you do, if you humble yourself and submit to the angel, then he will cause the rain that is caught up in the clouds to come down upon that grave and cool it, to wash away all your troubles and to restore all that was stolen from you: health, wealth, children, marriage, everything…'

He says many other things which they receive without questioning. He gives them three round pebbles that he instructs them to use, both of them; one with their drinking water and the remaining two each with their bath water early in the morning. They are to come to the church, or rather shrine, every Friday and Sunday henceforth, and they should get the other elders to lay their hands upon their heads so that they become true *mapostori*. They nod their heads in agreement.

'How much should we pay?' Mercy asks.

'Pay? Never ever say that in this place. This is holy ground, you should never mention money. Now, leave.'

'Thank you.'

'*Madzimai*,' he calls when they are just about getting up to their feet. They sit down again, and he continues. 'What is your name?'

'Mercy.'

'Your name is no longer Mercy. That one belongs to the synagogues. Your name henceforth is Purayirhodani. You will become a singer for the angels.'

'Thank you,' she says and begins to get up again. She doesn't like the name, but she has to agree. Omega said the man knows what he is doing, so she can't question it.

'You should come back here on Thursday next week, at six in the morning, alone, because the spirit needs you. You are very special.'

They leave the shrine with Tete still struggling to walk. Mercy does not know what to think of this or what Purayirhodani means, so she doesn't tell Omega of her new name or of her invitation to come back to the shrine. Neither does she mention any of it to Tinashe, who they find sleeping in the car as the day is gone and it is now a lot cooler.

Tinashe drives them back home, skipping gear number 3.

For the next few days, Mercy gives the water with the stones to Tete. She does not, during this time, engage in prostitution, partly because she does not have the time, and partly because she is still regurgitating Madzibaba Babylon's exhortation. When she thinks about it more, she does not really believe him and thinks that he is a conman. But, what boggles her mind is that he did not demand any money, as conmen should. All he gave them were free pebbles, and all they have to do is use water. What could ever go wrong with clean, clear water? It gives her a sense of confidence and purity. Not only that, but Tete believes that she is getting better, that the water is working as she sometimes is now able to sit for a long time. Mercy decides that she should go hear what the spirit has to say to her on Thursday.

Eighteen

Never again

'I will take you to the village in my car,' says Tinashe.

All he wants is to shield Tete from Madzibaba Babylon's shenanigans. He is also keenly aware that if she were to die in the city, Mercy would not be able to carry the burden.

'What about her belongings?'

'What belongings? I don't think it's worth talking about that.'

'But, why do you care Tinashe, what do you want from this? My love? Why do you keep coming after me as if there are no decent girls out there? Why won't you just leave me in peace?'

'I love you, Mercy. Truly. I know you made mistakes in the past, but I really don't care. I know you can change.'

'You know nothing about me, Tinashe. You don't know how many men have come through me. I am a prostitute, an *iwule*. *Hure remakoko*.'

'I don't care about that, Mercy. I don't even want to know. I believe in love, and I know that there is something between you and me. You know it.'

She truly doesn't understand this boy. Although she did feel something towards him at the beginning, before she started going after the pastors and the truck drivers, before she transformed herself into a proper prostitute, her heart has since been hardened. But this boy seems to be more possessed than in love, like he is just consumed with the idea of getting a 'yes' from her. He is too simple and too clean. His persistence frightens her.

'What if I have AIDS?' she asks, hoping to scare him away.

'I don't care Mercy, whatever you say. I know you don't have it, that deep down you are a good person. I knew you, way before you started all these your games. Besides, if you have it, then we can just find a way of living with it. Isn't there are ARVs these days?'

'Which are bloody expensive of course …'

'Trust me, Mercy. I have chased you for a long time. Surely, by now you know that I am the right guy. These your stories won't scare me away.'

'We will see, Tinashe. You are a good man. I am the bad girl, so I am doing you a favour here.'

She agrees eventually, to transfer Tete to the village. Tinashe will take them there in his ex-Japanese this Saturday, which means that Mercy can still visit Madzibaba Babylon on Thursday, to hear what the spirit has to say to her before she makes the trip. She won't tell Omega or Tinashe, she will just wake up in the morning and jump onto the bus. Tete is the only one who knows, if she still remembers anything.

On the Thursday, when she gets to the shrine, there are only two vehicles on the side of the road and one of them is just about driving away, leaving behind Madzibaba Babylon's white twin-cab. She jumps off the bus, which is on its way to Masvingo, and makes her way into the low-lying bushes where, from afar, she can see a bit of white close to the rocks. Madzibaba Babylon is there. She smiles. The quietness of the place scares her a little, so she utters a prayer in her breath as she walks at pace towards the place where Madzibaba Babylon ministered to them last week. She leaves her shoes by the bushes, not too far away from the place, and makes the remainder of the distance on bare feet.

She finds him kneeling on the ground, alone and shoeless, his head completely covered in a while veil with a red cross. She looks around; there is no one else, but them. She knows that she is on time, because when she got off the bus the radio said that it was five minutes to six. When she is closer to him, she sits down and waits for him to raise his head.

He is like that for a good time, bowed, before he slowly raises up his head. Then he smiles, exposing his white teeth. 'Ah, you came,' he says. 'I knew you would come. Please, come closer.'

Apprehensively, she draws a little closer and kneels at his feet. He reaches out to place his hands, both of them, on her perm which is covered in a white cloth. He says a lot of unintelligible words that she does not understand. He is talking to the spirit.

When he is done, she asks him, 'What did the spirit say?'

'I am still trying to connect, but the network is a bit of a problem. You see, there are lots of spirits in this area. Every day, they fight me, but I always win because I belong to the light. That light is shining upon you right now, *Madzimai*.'

'So, what's next? Will the spirit come back?'

'Just relax, *Madzimai* Purayirhodani,' he reassures her. 'The spirit comes when it wants. We just have to wait.'

They sit side by side for a few minutes, until he starts talking some nonsense. She tolerates him for a while, before the victim and the avenger in her springs up to life and stands erect, very much alert to what he could be up to in these bushes. However, as she is not sure, she gives him the benefit of the doubt. For now.

'*Madzimai*,' he says, 'You are not married. Am I right?'

'I am not.'

'You see now, *Madzimai*, before you came I was deep in prayer, and I saw you very clearly, your face. I asked the angel what you were doing in my presence, but he did not answer, he just showed me a girl who has not been very lucky with love. Does this mean anything to you, *Madzimai* Purayirhodani?'

'I have not been lucky with love.'

'You see now,' he smiles, 'that is why the spirit revealed to me a month before you showed up here, that it will be sending you my way. . I knew it the first time I saw you, that you are the one. You see, your face was not at all new to me, I had already seen you in the spirit.'

'What do you mean, *Madzibaba*?'

'What I mean, *Madzimai*, is that God has given me a gift of caring for women like you. You see, looking after six wives is a big job for many men, but for me, no, I do this very easily.'

'Why are you telling me this?'

'Oh come on, be grown up about this. The spirit already showed me; you in my kitchen, with many children, boys only, all handsome. .'

So, this douche-bag thinks that she can be his wife, she thinks. She will show him what she is made of.

'Are you crazy?' she says. 'You said the spirit wanted to talk to me, but now you are talking this nonsense. What is this?'

'You don't understand. *Madzimai* ...'

'What is it that I don't understand? That you are a thieving, womanising bastard just like the rest of them?'

'Don't insult the spirit ...'

'Which spirit? God's spirit or the devil's? Do you really know what you are talking about?'

She is up on her feet. And so is Madzibaba Babylon.

He grabs her by the arm, firmly. 'Listen,' he says, 'I don't want to force myself on you, but no one opposes the spirit, not you or anyone for that matter. Do you understand? Your being here in the first place, shows that you want it, otherwise why are you here, a woman, with a man in the bush? You want it. Just admit that you want it...'

'Let me go, please,' she says as she tries to pull away from him and as his hand and claws sink deeper into her skin. 'I will scream,' she continues.

'In this wilderness? You can cry all you like, but there is absolutely no-one that can stop me from doing what I want with you...'

'I will report you to the police.'

'Good luck with that. The commissioner is one of my members. And who would believe you anyway? You think I don't know that you give it to whoever wants it in the *shebeens*, huh? You think I did not read about you in the newspaper the other day?' He laughs as he says this, then continues, 'So, stop trying to be holy, Mercy. I can pay whatever you want, just like any of your other customers.'

'That's enough,' she screams and tries to wrestle her arm out of his grip. 'I sleep with whoever I choose to. I don't want to sleep with you, so let go of me!'

He grabs her by the waist and pulls her to himself so that her breasts rest on his chest. He tries to knock her feet off the ground using his bare right foot. She stumbles but doesn't fall as she continues holding on to his arm with her hand. She sinks her teeth into his left shoulder, tearing into him until she tastes the blood. He screams as they fall together onto the dust. He loosens his grip and she dives away, trying to get up to her feet and run away. But he won't allow this to happen. He grabs her by the ankle of her right leg and she comes back down, frantically kicking out at him with both legs and soiling his white rob. She catches him by the chin and he bites his tongue, blood immediately drooling from his mouth. He lets go of her, but when she gets up he is still trying to come after her, spitting the blood all over the place. She picks up a flat rock, the same one that Madzibaba Babylon pretended to sleep on and experience heavenly dreams the last time that she and Tete visited. She swings it at him with her might, catching his head just above the ear. He lets out a thud of a cry and suddenly goes quiet, blood coming out of his nostrils and mouth and a big wound dug into the side of his head. Motionless. A rush of cold grips Mercy. She kicks his tummy to find out if he is still conscious. He doesn't respond.

'I killed him,' she says to herself. 'I have killed a person.'

She panics, turns around and takes to her heels, barefooted, forgetting to pick up her shoes from the bushes. When she realises, she turns back to grab these, and as she does she notices a small movement from him. She turns away and resumes running without looking back until she is on the main road, then she runs along the tarred road towards Mutare, until she is out of breath. She starts walking, allowing several cars to whizz past her, until the truck driver who refused to pay her money a few years ago, stops for her. He doesn't recognise her.

'Do I know you from somewhere?' he asks when she is on board.

'I don't think so,' she says, avoiding his eyes and trying to disguise her voice.

'I sure met you before, but I just can't figure out where.'

'Maybe it's just resemblance.'

They are silent for a while as he concentrates on the road. She has already recognised him. She really never forgot him after that time. On another day, she would have tried to get revenge, but today she feels that if he can take her to town safely, he would have done enough to pay for her services that time.

'So, where are you coming from this early in the morning? And you look disturbed. Domestic matter, I guess?'

'Yes. My husband is in the army. He dumped me on the road.'

'Oh, sorry to hear that. But hey, these soldiers, they marry beautiful women to abuse like this? Such a shame.'

'They are like that, unfortunately. The last time he beat me and broke the leg of my friend because he thought that he was my boyfriend. He is the jealous type. He would kill for me, anytime.'

'Ey, hey! I better not mess up with this man of yours ...'

He doesn't say anything else until she drops off close to the Sakubva turn-off. He does not want anything to do with her. He decides that he better not get involved with the wrong people.

When Tinashe receives Mercy's call the following morning, he is confused. 'I don't understand, Mercy. We said tomorrow, so why do we now have to leave today. Besides, you know that I work today,' he says.

But she insists. 'If you love me, then you should take me and my aunt to the village, today.'

'But, why? What's happening?'

'She is getting worse and I don't want to risk it.'

'Alright then. Get ready. I will be there around two.'

It is today's headline in the Manica Post that propels her to this decision, the words of which are now inscribed on her memory like a deep tattoo: 'Madzibaba Babylon Dead.' The first time she sees it, she is combing the market in the morning for Tete's medicine, looking for a popular herb from India called *moringa,* which is selling like hot cakes. They say that it treats anything, which is good since the hospitals have no drugs most of the time. She stops herself from screaming out loud when she reads it on the board. All she does is turn back immediately and run back home without buying the drug. Although she knew that he could have died, she did not expect it to make the news. She planned to just forget about him, whatever happened to him, and to rub him off from her memory. But now, she thinks that she might have left evidence that could be linked back to her. No-one knows that she visited the shrine, but she just can't bank on that. She has to lie low in the village until it is all clear.

It is after 3pm when they set-off. The boot of the car and the passenger seat in the front are full of bags with Tete's own clothes and the remainder of her market stall. Mercy and Tete are sitting in the back, Tete lying on her lap all the time. She coughs now and again and groans and utters words that do not make sense. Mercy thinks that she is drifting away slowly. She can't wait to get to the village.

They arrive the village centre when it is already dark and the lights are on. Only the lights at the shops can be seen from afar as everywhere else is not electrified, just darkness and a few spots of red and amber from fires dotted around the village. Most of the villagers are having their supper at this time. Tinashe negotiates the dust road, normally used by scotch carts, with Mercy giving directions from the backseat. They go down the valley into Mupfurati, which is all dry and the white stones exposed, and out again, up the hill until they are on the tiny road from Mangwiro's house and the lights of the car are shining right into her father's yard, veering left, right and up, and drawing the attention of Father, Mother and Tribulation.

Mother and Father are worried. It does not happen often that they see a vehicle coming into their home, especially in the night, bearing good news. The last time that happened was many years ago, when Sekuru Chigodho's corpse was brought from the mortuary in the headmaster's car, for burial. The body had to lie in the house overnight before it was buried in afternoon of the morrow. Before that, the only other time was when Mangwiro returned from Marondera in his battered Peugeot which did not last the summer, and he had driven it all the way to their homestead to show it off.

'My daughter,' Mother says, rushing to the car as soon as Tinashe pulls the breaks. 'Is that you, my daughter?'

'Yes, *mama*. It is I.'

'Is everything okay where you are coming from?' Father asks as he follows behind Mother. They both look wasted; more than the last time Mercy saw them. They are old.

'Only a little, *baba*. Aunty is in the car and she is sick.'

They rush to the other side of the car as Tinashe slowly pulls himself out and no one pays attention to him, except for Tribulation. Tribulation drags his feet on the dust, walking on his hands as nobody thought to sit him in his wheelchair so he can move freely. Tinashe kneels next to him. 'How are you, young man?' he asks. 'You must be Tribulation?'

He nods his head.

'Well, I am happy to see you, finally,' he says as he pulls out a packet of candies from his trouser pockets.

Tribulation grabs this and immediately opens it, a broad smile painted across his face. Mercy observes this from the darkness, from the shadows where she is not confident enough to come out and meet her son. Mother and Father pull Tete out of the car and put her on the mattress in Mercy's hut, which is the one Tribulation has been using these days as he is now a big boy.

'Tribe,' Mercy says as she comes out of the shadows, attempting a smile.

'Mother,' he says, the broad smile still on his face. She is relieved.

'I missed you so much,' she says as she kneels down for a hug. 'You remember me, right, my son?'

'Yes, mother,' he says and starts crying. She cries with him until Father comes out of the hut and helps Tribulation up, and walks him into the kitchen together with everyone else.

After they are all seated and the introductions done, Father asks, 'So what is the problem with Tari?'

'I really don't know, *baba*. The doctors couldn't say.'

'That is strange. Is she bewitched then?'

'By who, *baba*?

'I don't know, but how can someone as young as her be so sick like she has AIDS? Surely, if she had it the doctors would have said, isn't that so Mai Mercy?'

'These days they don't say,' Mother says, 'they fear that you will all shun them, so they just say it is TB2.'

'I know,' Father says, 'but at least they say TB2, not that they can't see anything wrong.'

Mother prepares sorghum porridge mixed with some herbs and takes it to Tete. She feeds her like she is feeding a baby, until she has eaten it all. She is still churning out the nonsense, but at least now she has some energy.

After supper, they all retire to bed. Mercy sleeps with Tete in the hut whilst Tribulation sleeps in the kitchen and Tinashe in the car. When they are in their bedroom, Father and Mother debate whether Tinashe is just a friend of Mercy's or their future in-law.

Nineteen

Sekuru Godobori

It is in the morning. Tinashe is about setting off back to Mutare, and Mother is busy loading him with all sorts of village crops as goodwill. Mercy has already informed them that she will be staying in the village a little longer. Under normal circumstances, she would have been happy to have Mother relieve her of the heavy load of looking after Tete, and she would have jumped onto the next transport back to the city. But not this time. She is still haunted by the ghost of Madzibaba Babylon. It was never her intention, in as much as she has done a lot of bad things, to take away his life. The fact that this happened shakes her to the core. It makes her doubt whether she really controls her life or she is just floating about, tossed back and forth by forces higher than her, like a piece of wood. She is grateful though, to Tinashe, for his good heart. Now, she even thinks that it could work between them, that she should give them a try.

'Thank you so much, mother,' Tinashe says to Mother, respectfully, as he opens the door of the car, as Mercy jumps onto the passenger seat to accompany him to the village centre.

When he is gone, after Mercy accompanies him all the way to the village centre and tells him that she will consider his proposition and he bows down as if to worship her, Mother tells Mercy how he is such a fine young man, one that she should never lose. 'Does he go to church?' she asks.

'*Mama*, don't talk to me about your church business,' Mercy says. 'I have done that already, and I know that it is not by any means the standard of goodness.'

'But, you grew up in church, and if you really want to get married ...'

'I don't want to hear about it. Please.'

'Oh well, but that does not answer my question, does it?'

'Yes, he goes to church, but he is not my boyfriend. His going to church is not what makes him a good person.'

Mother ignores her. She takes the opportunity to explain to her how she needs God in order to overcome the witchcraft of the villagers, how Munamato would not have dumped her in the first place if it were not because of their jealousy neighbours. Mercy doesn't agree and puts the argument to bed by telling Mother to 'leave me alone and mind your own business.'

When the sun is well up, she visits the local clinic where Chipo now works as a nurse, the same one that many years ago the doctor made known of her pregnancy to those who were in the dark. She doesn't think much about that incident, her single aim is to make up with her friend and to laugh and reminisce about their childhood, about VaMusungwa and Freedom and Lovemore. She is not prepared, however, to talk about the pregnancy that produced her Tribulation. In as far as she is concerned, that issue is dead and buried. She has done much worse since she left the village, and worse has been done to her.

She finds Chipo sitting on a wooden bench on the veranda of the clinic, in her super-white uniform and cap.

'Oh my God!' exclaims Chipo when she sees her, 'Am I seeing clearly? Is that really you, Mercy?'

She runs to her and they embrace for a long time, then they unbuckle and look at each other and scream. Although she is still shorter, Chipo is no longer as little as she used to be, she has grown plump and full and her face has swelled a little.

'I can't believe this,' Chipo continues. 'Isn't it such an omen to see you here Mercy, in the village, a city girl like you?'

Mercy laughs, something she has not done in a long time, as they hold each other's hands, their hearts just as jubilant as when they were kids. 'What about you, Nurse Chipo?' she says. 'All white, huh? You even managed to send Nurse Mupunga packing. Nurse Chipo, heh-heh.'

They laugh their ribs out, both of them, as they sit on the bench. There are no patients around, just them and a male nurse wearing blue, who is busy mopping the cement floors with a cloth and water bucket. Mercy recognises him. He too, a long time ago, asked her out and she turned him down, swiftly. She felt insulted by it, to have been asked out by him. Chipo made fun of her because of it.

He smiles when he comes around to greet her. 'Mercy. Is that you?' he asks.

'Japhet, how are you? Do you work here as well?'

'Yes. Good heavens! Never thought we would see you again.'

'Here I am.'

He looks a little more handsome than he was back then, to put it nicely. At least he no longer wears the torn shorts he used to in school, so his ugliness is no longer as pronounced. When he goes back to his mopping, after a brief chat, Mercy and Chipo have a good, long, stifled laugh, giggling under their breath so he doesn't notice that they are laughing at him.

'Would you love him now,' asks Chipo, 'if he were to ask?'

'You are a crazy woman, Nurse Chipo. He is your man. Who knows what you two are up to in this clinic when no one is looking ...?'

'Iii, *vasikana*, leave me alone …'

'But, seriously, he is really not that bad, come to think of it…'

'Well, looks like you have travelled all the way from the city to find your man, Mercy,' Chipo laughs.

'Look at you Chipo. You pray for a husband and God grants you one, then you ignore him … ha ha! Anyway, who are you with now, since you dumped your sweetheart, Lovemore? You are getting old my friend …'

'Look at the kettle. Calling the pot black, heh? You are the beautiful one, so tell me when you are getting married. As for me, I am waiting for you to go first.'

Although they laugh about it, Mercy knows that it is true that they are getting old. By the standards of the village, they should either be married now or at least be in the process, unless there is something seriously wrong with them. It doesn't concern her much, however, because she doesn't believe in marriage anymore. And if she changes her mind, she can always get married to Tinashe. After all, Omega was right that marriage is highly overrated and, of course, love is a myth. 'I will not get married,' she says.

'You just didn't say that, Mercy. Why?'

'I have seen the world and am now wiser. That is why. For me, no marriage.'

'Iii, *vasikana*, how times change. You are the one who wanted to have a church wedding that would bring the whole village to a halt, in a long white gown with laces, and now you don't want to get married?'

'Do you, Chipo? Do you want it?'

'Of course. It's the natural thing.'

'Then, what is the problem?'

'I don't know, Mercy, but one thing that I am sure about is that there is something wrong in our families, at least in mine. Most of our agemates are now gone, all married, even the ugly ones. Except, of course, for those who do not want to get married like you, and the unfortunate ones like me. You remember Aunty Rhoda, do you, the one who left a long time ago to go to Zambia?'

'Of course, I remember her. We were small kids then.'

'Well, she came back, can you believe it, old and sick. Not married. Never married. Just like your aunt, Tarisayi, how is she now?'

'I came with her. She is not feeling well ...'

'You see, Mercy? That is why I think we are bewitched. How come none of us gets married? Look around the whole clan, even Babamunini Pemberai's daughters, wherever they are in the farms, none of them is married.'

Mercy thinks about it, then says, 'Are you telling me that men are not chasing after you?'

'They do Mercy, but all they ever want is sex. And the good ones never come. I am tired of this whole waiting business. Sometimes I feel like just getting myself pregnant, to acquire a child of my own.'

'I know what you mean ...'

'Is it the same for you, Mercy? Even you?'

Mercy doesn't respond. She is deep in thought.

That Mercy, as beautiful as she is, is also struggling to pin down a man, gives Chipo more reason to believe that something indeed is wrong. 'You see what I am talking about?' she continues. 'We have been bewitched ...'

'No way, Chipo. There is no witchcraft. It doesn't exist. Yes, men have abused me, but most of the time it was my fault, my choice ...'

'You don't know what you are talking about, something must have happened for you to get to that point in the first place.'

'Listen, Chipo. I am not that little, innocent, virgin girl anymore. I have seen a lot in the city ...'

Mercy opens up to her, starting with Biggie up until Pastor Goodness and Tinashe, and Omega and Mati. She deliberately avoids talking about Father and Tribulation. She has learnt over the years, to avoid talking about that portion of her life. It is as if it never happened, as if Tribulation just fell from the sky. She also doesn't talk about Madzibaba Babylon. Her chest thumps against her ribs when she thinks about him. That one is her secret for life, she will never mention it to anyone. 'I have been a bad girl Chipo. But such is life,' she concludes.

Chipo is stunned. Dumbfounded. Her jaw is dropped, her mouth gaping, words refusing to come out of her. 'Mercy,' she finally says, but stops right there. She hugs her hard and finds tears rolling down her face. 'I am sorry,' she continues.

'Don't be sorry for me,' Mercy says. Unmoved.

'I also have a story to tell you, now that you have poured out your heart. This will shock you.'

'What?'

'It's about my father.'

'Your father?'

'It is because of him that my mother died when we were kids. So, all along, all this hard life and heartache, it is because of him. And you know, Mercy, he also abused Francis all these years, from when he was a toddler. He sodomised him ... can you believe it?'

'Really? Your brother? Iii, Mangwiro. I knew about your mother. He beat her isn't it, and drove her to commit suicide. But Francis, iii, I never thought your father could do such a thing...'

Chipo is in tears, 'Francis only told me this, three months ago, and I have grappled with it ever since. He can't live with it anymore, and I am struggling. How do I even ask him, Mercy, how? Francis ran away from the house last week. He is a troubled boy.'

'So, where is he now?'

'Who knows? But it got me thinking about everything, why anyone would do anything like that, and about all this marriage thing. All of that. I think my father has a *chikwambo*, a goblin that causes him to do all these things.'

Chipo's story unravels Mercy's fragile peace. Why did Father rape her? That question has never been answered. She has always sought to avoid it, to burry this all under the carpet. She thought she was doing well. Until now.

Does Father also have a *chikwambo*? Could all this bad luck that has followed her be linked to this creature? It bothers her.

'What are you thinking?' asks Chipo.

Mercy is crying. She has not done so in a long time. She feels anger build up inside of her, the same kind that she had towards Munamato after he jilted her. Now, she thinks that the real person who jilted her, that set her on this path in the first place, is Father. Why did he rape her? The question now requires an answer. She leans against Chipo's shoulder, like a child.

Japhet comes around to find out what's happening. 'What's the matter?' he asks.

Chipo motions with her hand for him to go away. He disappears into the children's area, baffled.

'He raped me,' Mercy says.

'Your father?'

She nods her head.

'I knew it. These bastards. I knew it all along, Mercy. It was obvious to me. What's wrong with these people?'

Chipo suggests that they visit a witchdoctor, a *n'anga* who lives near the commercial farming district, in Dorowera, to get some answers. 'We have to be cleansed,' she says.

Mercy is reluctant. Spiritism has never worked for her. Every time, those who claimed to commune with the supernatural have disappointed her. But Chipo is so convinced and so, for her sake, she agrees. They will do it on Monday, when Chipo is off duty. They have to test the hypothesis put forward by her, that they are bewitched. They have to be sure. They have to do this before their fathers' goblins destroy their lives completely. Besides, Mercy wants to know why Father raped her. She needs to know, urgently.

On Monday, they jump onto the bus to the growth point in the early hours of the morning, after tea. They wait at the growth point for a good two hours for the truck that goes to Dorowera. They have to get the truck, otherwise would have to wait for the lone bus that goes there on its way from Harare, which departs the growth point around 8pm.

They are in the Dorowera area by 1pm and, after jumping off the truck at the 'big rock,' they are directed to Sekuru Godobori's residence by one little boy who is looking after his father's goats in the vast forest. There are not many settlements close to the bus stop or any sign of civilisation, apart from the dust road which cuts through the forest, meandering between the mountains and the hills, crossing over several small bridges that can only fit one vehicle at a time.

As they make their way through the thicket, following the paths used by herdsmen and going along the small tributary river that is almost drying up, they grab some purple and red berries along the river bank and say very little to each other, each debating in their own mind what exactly they expect to hear from Sekuru Godobori. When they reach where the tributary empties into the main river, and the thicket becomes more dispersed and less frightening, they see a few settlements. Sekuru Godobori's homestead, according to the young boy's directions, is the one with the many huts enclosed in a wall of poles and sticks neatly weaved together like a mat.

When they are closer, a few dogs run towards them, barking and their tails erect, sending shivers up Chipo's spine. They stand still and the dogs all rush back into the enclosure, just as one little man, a midget, comes out to open the wooden gate for them.

'Greetings, ladies,' he says in a deep voice, too big for his size.

'Greetings,' they say as they bend their legs and clasp their hands together in the manner of women.

'Is this Sekuru Godobori's place?' Chipo asks.

'Very well so, my lady. Please, come this way.'

There are a few other people in the yard all waiting to see the old man, Sekuru Godobori, seated in clusters that Chipo guesses are groups of families. None of them has shoes on their feet, and the men have their pants folded from their ankles up to the knees, as if they are about to wade through a river that is half-full.

'No shiny things, please,' says the midget when they are close to the isolated hut that is Sekuru Godobori's surgery. 'If you have any phones, rings, bangles, earrings, watches or anything shiny, then you better leave them here,' he says as he motions his hands, directing them to a place on some rocks in the yard, where the other people left their stuff scattered around. 'And no shoes,' he continues.

The girls strip themselves of all things shiny, leaving only their clothes and underwear, and after about an hour, they are let in to see Sekuru Godobori.

Before they can sit down, Sekuru Godobori shakes his head several times, like a goat, and says, 'I knew you would come. It was time. You are from my old friend, Kamutsi's area, isn't it? May the ancestors rest his spirit in peace.'

Mercy is surprised by this. How does he know? she wonders. She looks around the hut, which is dark and full of smoke which tears her eyes despite her having grown up in the village. Hung around its edges are many artefacts, including a lion's head, shiny python skin and other weird stuff she does not recognise. There is another man, another midget, sitting next to Sekuru Godobori, identical to the one they met outside. Like Sekuru Godobori, he is adorned in greasy traditional wear: a piece of animal skin tied around the waist to cover only the essential parts, like in the pictures of Nehanda Nyakasikana and Sekuru Kaguvi which Mercy is quite familiar with from the history books. Apart from this, he and Sekuru Godobori essentially have no other clothes on them. Mercy could swear that they do not have underwear underneath the animal skins, she can see a lot of black and brown when the midget dances around like one who is possessed. Pencilled on their faces are decorations of red and white, as if made of white chalk and red paint. Sekuru

Godobori also has a crown of feathers on his bald head and more drawings around his eyes. In his right hand, he holds a tiny broomstick that looks like the tail-end of a dead cow wound around a chicken's leg. He dips it into some substance in a clay water pot, just as Chipo and Mercy take their seats on the floor and bow their heads. He sprinkles the substance into their face with the broomstick, the midget growling like a dog, making some frightening sounds.

Sekuru Godobori fills his mouth with water from a calabash, then spits it out, vehemently, splashing it into the girls' faces. They do not wipe it, they know that doing so would be disrespectful.

'I know why you are here,' he continues. 'You want some answers.'

He looks at Mercy and says, 'You, you will never get married. Your father has a goblin, a *chikwambo* which I gave to him because he wanted to be rich. He was supposed to sleep with you, that was the condition, and to bring you here to serve the gods for a year. He was not supposed to sleep with your mother during that time. But he is a weak man. He couldn't obey all the requirements. He will die a pauper. Shame on him.'

Mercy is surprised by how the old man seems to know so much without even asking. It is true, what Chipo said. 'You mean to say that my father agreed to sleep with me so he can be rich?' she asks.

'Of course, why else? But he chickened out. He disrespected the spirit. Yes, Petros is a chicken, and his ancestors must be ashamed of him.'

'What about my mother? Did she have anything to do with that?'

'What did you think, girl? They came together, they promised that they will go through with everything. But they didn't. They wanted to take short cuts, but there is nothing like that, these things have no reverse. The *chikwambo* that your father has, it is your husband. There is no way out of this.'

The words sink into Mercy like a knife, slowly.

She bursts out in tears.

Chipo is the same. Sekuru Godobori tells her all about Mangwiro and Francis and their mother with striking detail. It surprises them that although Sekuru Godobori claims to have been involved in most of this, he seems to have no regrets whatsoever. He has to do whatever his clients request of him, he says, so he is not the one to blame. At least Chipo is not bewitched, according to him, although she will now have to come back with Francis in order for her luck to change. Francis will have to serve at Sekuru Godobori's shrine for a year, otherwise his life will be ridden with bad luck.

Mercy's anger is rekindled, not against Sekuru Godobori, but against her parents. What troubles her most, is Mother. How could she do that to her? How could she connive with Father to harm her like that and still pride herself as leader of the RW? All the tears and the sympathy from her, yet all along she knew why Father raped her.

Now, it is clear that all that happened to her, including the rape, is because of his parents' desire to be rich. They were happy to crucify her as long as they ended up with more goats and cows. The veil has been removed. Her eyes have been opened. If she had finished school and not had a baby, if she had not as a result gone to Mutare and made herself vulnerable to all the men who took advantage of her, if she had a normal youth and was given a chance to be normal, perhaps she wouldn't be in this situation. She wouldn't even be in this terrible place right now. Indignation rising inside of her, in a huff she gets up to her feet and storms out of the hut, Chipo is pursuit, before Sekuru Godobori could finish talking about the remedy.

'Come back, hey. Come back,' the two midgets run after them.

'Sekuru has not yet given you permission to leave,' says one of the midgets. 'If you leave like this, you will be cursed.'

Mercy does not look back. Neither does she care.

Chipo runs after her, looking back as she does.

As they are on the path cutting through the forest, Mercy is now running, as if someone is pursuing her. Chipo follows behind, struggling to keep up with her. The herdsmen coming back to the village at the end of the day, as the sun is about setting, look at them with amusement.

When they hit the road, they do not stop at the 'big rock' but continue walking in the direction of the growth point, which is tens of miles away. Despite Chipo's efforts, Mercy does not at all say a word. She is too full.

Twenty

Hurricane

They arrive at the village centre at midnight, aboard a noisy tractor transporting produce from the farms to the remote villages by the border, driven by one old man who found them walking on the dusty road from the growth point, who sings at the top of his voice as the tractor edges forward like a tortoise. If it were not because of him and because of the white farmer who carried them on his motorbike from Dorowera to the growth point, they would surely be spending the night with the crickets in the jungle. The white farmer who gave them the lift, Mr Thompson, is only but one of a handful left in the country after many of his kinsmen who refused to toe the line were kicked out by the rulers. He is well known and liked in the district, very much integrated into the society that the villagers no longer see his colour. He is one of them.

'Don't do it, Mercy,' Chipo says after they drop off and have passed by Mangwiro's compound, as she follows behind Mercy on the path from there in tears. 'It's not worth it.'

'Go back home, Chipo,' Mercy says in a voice which is stern and harsh. Determined. 'This is none of your business. It is between my parents and ...'

'Please, Mercy, you are my friend ...'

Chipo begs, but Mercy isn't listening. She cannot be stopped. The more she thinks about it, the more she rages on the inside. Anger surges up inside her and a rush of blood floods her brain. Wielding an axe which moments ago she grabbed from the edge of Mangwiro's hut, which was hung just under the thatched roof by the door, and with her left hand clutching a five-litre plastic container full of petrol from Mangwiro's workshop, she is like a jihadist bride on a holy mission. A hurricane. Chipo's begging only but adds fuel to the fire. Brandishing the axe as if she is to slash off Chipo's nose with it, she turns towards her and says, 'Mind your own business, Chipo.'

For a moment, Chipo is frozen, and noticing the seriousness in her friend's voice, she runs back home to alert Mangwiro.

Mercy does not waste any time. When she arrives at her father's homestead, she is shouting at the top of her voice like a drunkard. Tete is fast asleep in the girls' hut, Tribulation in the kitchen. Mother and Father are in their hut, lost in fuzzy sleepy lands. She grabs from the wooden plates rack in the yard, a hard rope which is normally used by Father to stabilise the cows when he robs them of their children's milk in the morning. She secures the bedroom door from the outside with the rope, grabs the ladder from behind Father and Mother's hut and rests it against the thatch, then climbs onto it with the five-litre container in her hand. She does to this side of the square hut what she does to the others, pouring the petrol and soaking the thatch in it.

It is too late when Father wakes up, his nostrils full of the smell of petrol. He can hear Mercy shouting, 'You will die today, Petros, you will die.' He shakes Mother to wake her up, and she jerks up and sits on the bed. 'What is it?' she asks, rubbing her eyes with her angles in a sleepy way. Then she looks up at Father who is now wrestling with the door as he tries to break it open from the inside.

Mercy's voice thunders through the atmosphere, like the early rains. 'Today, you will meet with your maker,' she fumes. 'Both of you. How could you? How dare you do that to me? You decide to sacrifice me, heh, for what? Where is the love, *baba*, *mama*? For what? For wealth, to have me crippled for life, to rob me of my own life. All along I thought it was me who did wrong, that there was something wrong with me, but now my eyes have opened. I used to think that I was useless, but no, you are just an evil pair. You bastards messed me up, but today it ends, right here and right now ...'

She lights up a bunch of dry grass in her left hand, soaked in petrol, with a cigarette lighter, holding the axe in her right hand and tears rolling down her cheeks.

Tete is up and has crawled to the door of her hut, but she can't speak or do anything. She is weak. The whole thing is unfolding before her eyes like a dream, like it is really not happening. Tribulation also has crawled to the door of the kitchen hut. He is crying as Father and Mother shout from the inside their hut.

'Mercy, my daughter. Please open the door and let us talk,' begs Father.

'What about me, my daughter, what have I done?' cries Mother.

'Yes, what has your mother done?' Father asks. 'If you want revenge, then I am your man, but please let your mother live. She doesn't deserve this. Mercy, my daughter, please have mercy upon your mother. You can do whatever you want with me.'

'Shut up!' cries Mercy. 'You will explain that to your maker, not me. I am fed up with all your lies. And you, *mama*, you are a disgrace to womanhood. Your *n'anga* told me everything. I know you were there, so stop playing innocent.'

Waking up to the fact that she is never going to lend them an ear, Father begins ramming himself against the door from the inside, together with Mother. But it is too late. Mercy torches up the roof and the liquid agrees with the flame, spreading quickly with the help of the wind. In a moment, the room is filled with smoke as the fire cracks through the dry roof. Father grabs the axe that he keeps under the bed and starts chopping at the wooden door, frantically, as Tete's tears flow silently and Tribulation cries in a hoarse voice.

When Mangwiro and Chipo arrive in the yard, running, Father and Mother are just jolting out of the raging fire after the door comes down and the roof is just falling in, and many other villagers are rushing to the homestead. Father's, and Mother's, clothes are on fire and their screams cutting through the atmosphere with terror. Father rolls himself on the sand to put out the flame, but Mother runs towards the path that goes to the cattle pens, adding more oxygen to the fire and causing the flame to blow up. Mangwiro runs after her and tackles her to the ground, rolling on the ground with her and his own clothes sticking against hers. He uses his shirt to put out the fire from her perm.

Meanwhile, Mercy inflicts a big dig into Father's face with the axe, cutting across the left side of his nose and mouth. She is about to have a second slice when one of their neighbours, a man, grabs the axe before she swings it forwards from her back, holding it by the blade and cutting the inside skin of his hands. She falls to the ground together with him and loses her grip. They both jolt up to their knees and make a dash for the axe, bumping their heads in the dust before Chipo pulls it away and tosses it into the raging fire.

In no time, the homestead is full of people.

Mercy is breathing high and sobbing. The men have tied her hands from behind, but she won't talk to them or answer their questions as she sits by the kitchen door, subdued and Tribulation clinging to her. They decide to take her and Chipo to the chief's compound for the remainder of the night as Mangwiro takes Tribulation and Tete to his home, carrying Tribulation on his back and one of the men pushing the wheelbarrow Tete is in.

Meanwhile, Father and Mother are loaded onto one businessman's vehicle and are taken to the district hospital, the same one where Mercy was taken many years ago, after she tried to kill herself because of the very thing that is now dogging them.

On the morrow, the police are present at Chief Chisindi's court. Chipo, like back then in Chief Kamutsi's court, explains everything to them, including all about Mangwiro and his abuse of Francis. Mangwiro denies everything but, despite him being one of the elders in the chief's palace, the police leave with him and Mercy in chains. The matter will now be dealt with by a magistrate.

The villagers are shocked. And so is Reverend Mbudzi. He just cannot believe that Mother did such a thing. She has been such as a champion of women, a beacon of light shining in the community, which is why he has recently been campaigning for her reinstatement as leader of the

RW following the departure of Nurse Mupunga to work at the district hospital.

The story is the talk of the village and beyond, and has attracted media attention from throughout the country. The journalists visit the village and the growth point with their big trucks and dishes, with their pens and microphones and notepads. Mapudege is quoted by many of the them, saying that she has always viewed Mother and Father with suspicion, that she is not surprised that they did such a thing. They have always been weird.

Mercy does not deny any of the charges brought against her: grievous bodily harm and attempted murder. She is happy to serve her time in jail, or to even die. It is not as if she looks forward to life after all, in jail or out of it. In as far as she is concerned, there really is nothing to live for, not even Tribulation who is actually a constant reminder of what she has gone through over the years, who is to her a brother and a son at the same time. She owns up to everything and, after the trial, she is slapped with a ten-year sentence, four years of which are suspended in light of the injustices committed against her and on condition of her not committing a similar crime in the future.

When she is sentenced, Tinashe is in the court, tears bathing his face. He shakes his head and looks at her with a load of mercy and sorrow. It dawns on him that the romance he entertained in his head has now come to an abrupt end, that his fantastical hope of changing Mercy was what it was, a fantasy. It occurs to him how indeed he had no clue who Mercy really was, what she has gone through over the years. He was and is still too removed from the experience to be able to reach deep into her heart. He does not wait to see her driven to the provincial prison in the grey prison truck.

Mangwiro, on the other hand, does not go to trial. His case is postponed as the victim is not present. He is remanded out of custody until Francis is found, which happens eventually. The herdsmen find his remains after many days, fully decomposed and lying along the bank of Mupfurati. Mangwiro continues to deny the charges against him and, in the end, the state fails to prove its case. He is acquitted of the crime, but Chipo refuses to continue living in the same house as him. She relocates to Harare and finds a job at Parirenyatwa Hospital. She vows to never set her feet in the village again.

Father and Mother are recovering in the hospital, under guard from the police. Mother's burns are deeper than Father's, but Father is lucky to survive, albeit with a deformed nose and mouth from the dig dug across his face by Mercy. Both of them weep all the time, for their daughter who is now in prison, and for their own sins which have brought them to this point. It does not get better for them when Tete passes away in her sleep in Mangwiro's house. They are not present when she is buried next to Sekuru Chigodho's grave, in a spot that Father cleared for his own self sometime time ago, as if he knew that it would be required this soon. When he learns of her death, he envies her, he wishes that he had died instead of her.

'Sir,' Father says to the policeman guarding him, 'my daughter is innocent. Whatever she did, it was because I drove her to do it. I deserve to be in that jail. I deserve everything that has happened to me, but my daughter is just a victim. Please, sir, is there a way that my daughter can be released, if I confess?'

'No,' says the policeman, 'that is not possible. Your daughter committed her own crimes by trying to kill you and your wife. She will have to serve her own time.'

Father begs the policeman every day until he no longer responds to his pleas. He just ignores him, for the begging is too much.

Father is happy when the time of their trial comes. He and Mother are driven to the court in the same truck. It is the first time they see each other since the fire as they have been in different wards. They are seated in the back of the truck, silently at first, with two armed guards wearing green uniform and sturdy brown boots.

'How are you holding up?' Father finally asks Mother.

Her response is crying.

'I am sorry, my love,' he continues. 'All that I wanted was to provide for you, to give you a better life. In this, I have utterly failed.'

'I told you, Petros, I told you but you wouldn't listen,' cries Mother. 'I told you that this Sekuru Godobori of yours will get us into trouble.'

'I know, my wife, I know. I was wrong, you were right, so now I have to pay. I will fight for you my wife. It was I that did this, not you.'

They cry until they reach the gate, to a scramble media people wanting to photograph their faces. They wipe off their tears.

The trial does not take long as they both accept their crimes. In the end, Mother is acquitted as she did not participate in the rape. She gets away with a suspended sentence and a fine for covering up Father's crime, but Father is slapped by the no-nonsense female magistrate with nine years of hard labour. He is taken to a prison in Harare.

Twenty-one

Previous

When the iron gates close behind her and she is dressed in the yellow uniform now turned khaki, when she enters the smelly corridor and all eyes are fixed on her and the other prisoners hurl insults at her, when she enters the cell that has a defecating bucket in one corner into which they empty their bowls during the night, which usually fills up very quickly and spills over, when Big Maria sneers at her like she is a piece of s**t, Mercy knows that she is now beyond redemption. It is not any better on the outside, yet still, the cold reception that she receives grants her a more definitive identity of who she has become: a criminal.

The skinny female guard who brings her, who is dressed in a green uniform and looks just as miserable and malnourished as the prisoners, closes the heavy metal door and clips the huge locks that bring together the heavy chains, smiles at her knowingly and walks away. Mercy looks around. There are many black faces pasted around the iron bars and there is an overwhelming stench emanating from there which hits her like a dead animal's perfume, exacerbated by unbathed armpits and reused underwear pads.

'Welcome, boy!' says Big Maria, her oversized breasts rubbing against Mercy's face as she immediately asserts her authority, towering high above her, the atmosphere full of her presence. The other cellmates laugh, sarcastically.

'What brings you here, pretty one?' continues Big Maria.

Mercy is not sure how to respond, whether she should say anything at all. She stands by the entrance, just on the inside of the locked cell which is supposed to hold four but now has nine, holding in her hand a thin red blanket and shivering from the cold. She doesn't say a word, even as Big Maria pokes her on the forehead with her hard index finger which is big like Biggie's. 'Say something, b***h! You are not a saint or anything, but a criminal like all of us. The earlier you understand who is in charge here, the better it will be for you,' she says.

Still, Mercy doesn't say a thing. She stands there, timid, as Big Maria pushes her against the steel bars and bangs her shaved head against the metal, grabs her by the collar and lifts her in one hand by the neck. Keeping her cool on the outside, Mercy tells herself that she shouldn't show any sign of weakness, that silence is better than begging for mercy. Big Maria lets go of her and she thuds to the ground like an overripe *bhuru-mango* fruit, much to the ululation of her cellmates and inmates in the other cells. Picking herself up, Mercy attempts to walk to a corner of the cell where there is a bit of space. There are no beds in the cell; the prisoners sleep on the cement floor.

'Where do you think you're going, b***h?' Big Maria asks as she grabs her from behind and pushes. Still, Mercy doesn't cry or say anything. She sits there, on the cement floor, as Big Maria and the others have a good laugh. Big Maria walks into the space in the corner, which could fit two people comfortably.

'Maybe she is dumb,' says Nyarai, a skinny and short woman Mercy figures she could squash flat just by sitting onto.

'She is mine tonight,' another of the cellmates, Pams, says. 'Is that okay, Big M?'

'No,' says Big Maria, 'this one is fresh meat. Too fresh for you. Only I should have her, unless you ae willing to pay, Ms Pams.'

'Of course, Big M ...'

'So can I,' says Nyarai.

'Well, she goes to the highest bidder,' Big Maria decides. 'Five cigarettes for an hour with the newbie...'

They bid and outbid each other as Mercy continues sitting on the floor. They are excited and cold, except for Previous, who remains in her corner, close to the bucket, reading a book in the dim light. Pams outbid them all, but Big Maria overrules her and decides that she will sleep with Mercy herself, that she will use her as the extra blanket that she needs to keep herself warm in the chilly weather.

When the lights go out and they arrange themselves to sleep in two rows like sacks, squashed up in the small cell except for Big Maria who has enough space in her corner, which is furthest from the bucket, Mercy is still sitting close to the entrance and Big Maria bidding her to come join her unless she wants to stay up the whole night. By remaining silent, Mercy chooses the later, so Big Maria snatches the red blanket from her. Mercy does not protest. She waits until they all are asleep and Nyarai has moved from her place and tucked herself into Big Maria's blankets, then she puts down her head against the urine-splattered cement floor, next to Previous and closest to the bucket. There, she tries to catch a sleep or two with virtually no success, Previous watching her in the darkness as she twists and turns and bundles herself together into an S-shape in the cold. How could she find any sleep with all the bad air exuded by Big Maria and Nyarai throughout the night as they make little noises and take turns to defecate in the bucket which is already full.

In the morning, they are let out into the open eating area in the middle of the prison blocks and handed the aluminium cups and plates. This reminds Mercy of her time with MaNcube in the mines, how the miners admired her and fancied themselves with her. She remembers MaNcube's kindness and smiles to herself at the thought of it, until Previous interrupts her.

'What's making you smile, sister?' asks Previous.

'Nothing.'

'You should just ignore those stupid girls if you want to survive in this place. Like you did last night.'

'Thank you.'

After collecting their food; white mealie-meal porridge and black tea with no sugar, they sit on the floor, in a corner since almost all benches are already occupied. Big Maria is sitting a few meters away, with Nyarai and Pams and a few other girls, casting their eyes at the pair and laughing at them.

'They are mischievous, those girls,' says Previous, 'but if you show them that you are not moved by their threats they will back off ... Anyway, what did a pretty girl like you do to be in here?'

'I killed people,' says Mercy. She decides to portray herself as a very cold case, one that another should never mess up with, a trick which Mati told her back in Mutare, which Mati used when she was on the inside. It is not entirely untrue, however, considering that Mercy did actually kill Madzibaba Babylon.

Previous is shocked by the revelation, very much. How could a girl so pretty do anything like that? 'Oh, I see. That makes you the most dangerous in our cell then,' she says.

'Why?'

'Well, Big M is in for robbery, and Pams for abusing a small boy. None of these guys has done anything as serious, you know. How did you kill them? Were they men?'

'A man. And a woman. I chopped them into small pieces with an axe.'

The news spread after that, but Big Maria refuses to buy it, until she speaks to one of the guards who, out of wanting to annoy her, adds that after killing the man and the woman, Mercy actually ate some of their flesh.

'So, why is she in this section?' asks Big Maria.

'Stop asking stupid questions, Maria,' is the answer. 'That is none of your business.'

That is enough for Big Maria and the other bullies to leave Mercy alone, for now.

Mercy strikes a friendship with Previous, who is the saner of them all, and strikes more fear into Big Maria and crew by refusing to take any of their orders to empty the bucket into the pit latrine behind the prison blocks, which they share with the male section, or to do any of the chores such as scrubbing the smelly floors of the cell. Instead, she is more vocal with time, openly challenging anyone who dares touch Previous or her, and getting into a fight with one girl when they are busy digging the fields, swinging a pick which catches and amputates the other girl's toe. Slowly, she becomes one of the prison queens although inwardly she is still terrified. Big Maria stays away, but she still is not fully convinced and continues to watch her like a hawk.

'What's that book you are always reading in the night?' asks Mercy.

'My bible,' Previous replies.

'Bible?'

'Yes. The church-people come every Tuesday, in the small hall. Do you want to come with me one of the days?'

'No, I don't.'

The 'church-people'. They seem to follow her wherever she goes, and she doesn't like it. But she does notice the smile on Previous's face, how she seems to cope with everything despite the abuse. She wonders how she manages it. She knows now that Previous has been in prison for a long time, after she poisoned her husband for cheating on her with her little sister. For that, Mercy respects her, she feels that she should have done the same to Munamato for what he did to her, and to Father for laying down the foundation of her abuse, for drilling the hole which was used by all the other robbers to plunder her goods. Poisoning them would probably have given her satisfaction and more of a sense of closure. The fact that Father is rotting away in a prison somewhere does not do it for her. Every day that passes, she is convinced that she would not have been in this situation had it not been because of him.

'Can I talk to you, about Jesus?' Previous asks, kindly.

'And what exactly would you talk to me about that poor man?'

'Love. Just love.'

Mercy laughs and does not hide her sarcasm, 'You don't know what you are talking about, Previous. Ask me and I will tell you all about this Jesus of yours.'

'Talk to me then. About this man.'

'Firstly,' Mercy begins, 'he doesn't exist. Not only that, but even the people who told you about him do not actually believe so themselves. It is just a game, my friend, a profession. You see, I grew up in church, and I even dated pastors, several of them, including married ones. None of them was genuine. I have seen enough to know that this God of yours actually does not exist.'

'Well, that is your experience. Mine is the opposite. I never saw the door of a church until I was in prison ...'

'You see. You are vulnerable, that's why ...'

Despite Previous's efforts, Mercy is not moved. She is convinced that religion is just a waste of time, although Previous's consistently good attitude does bother her a little, just like Tinashe's kindness did. Previous is always positive and smiling and is granted all sorts of favours by the guards, like being asked to clean the offices and floors when everyone else is busy sweating in the fields. There is something about her that is unsettling, something that is too good to be true. Mercy is convinced, however, that Previous is inexperienced in the matters of life, that with time she too will become just as disillusioned with this whole thing as she is.

On a Saturday, after many months on the inside, Mercy is told that she has some visitors. The only people who have visited her and only in the early days of her incarceration, are Mother and Tinashe. At those times, she refused to talk to Mother, all the nine times that she came. And Tinashe, poor handsome Tinashe, she only spoke to him twice, both times leaving him sitting on the stool on the other side of the bars, abruptly, after he veered off talking about this Jesus nonsense Previous is so obsessed with. It is obvious to her that there will never be a romantic relationship between them, that all Tinashe now wants is to brainwash her with this 'good news'. She made it clear after the second attempt that she will never meet him again.

As she walks towards the visitors' booth, she can see Reverend Mbudzi and Chipo on the other side, from afar, and, for a moment, she thinks of running back to her cell. She is happy to see Chipo, but is not at all comfortable seeing Reverend Mbudzi. He is too straight forward a man, unlike the others, as if this religion of his is actually true. She feels judged by him. It was not always like this for her, for she used to like him and his wife, a lot, when life was all sweet and simple, until Munamato ditched her and she became convinced that they are all the same, that Reverend Mbudzi is just too good at acting. Thus, she has avoided him, even after she moved back to the village from the city. But now, he is sitting there with a broad smile as she walks towards the stool in her yellow uniform. She takes her seat on the inside of the iron bars, on the stool, unsmiling and embarrassed.

'How are you, my daughter?' Reverend Mbudzi says after a long silence.

She doesn't look up, but says in a subdued voice, 'Fine.'

Then there is another long pause, before he says, 'How are you keeping up? Are you taking good care of yourself?'

'Yes,' she replies, looking up into his cool eyes. 'But, it's difficult.'

'I can imagine. Which is why I am here. I came just to let you know that I understand what you are going through, that all is not lost.'

'No. You don't understand,' she snaps.

'Believe me, daughter. I do. I have seen enough people in similar situations. So, at least from that perspective, I do understand. You see, daughter, life is like this. Things happen to us that we regret, some because of our fault, others because of other people's faults. But our God, he is the Lord of mercy, he loves us all the same.'

'Love, Reverend. There is nothing like love.'

'Don't say that, Mercy. Remember the Christ, what he went through. He died for you.'

'Reverend, there is no Christ. Where was he when all these things happened to me? Where was God when the Christ was killed? If he couldn't do anything for his son, then why is he god at all?'

Reverend Mbudzi ponders, then says, 'Listen, Mercy. I know you are hurting. I know that there is no undoing what happened to you. But, you see, life is a journey, we make choices and our choices affect not only us, but other people too. Our choices become our life. Sometimes we are victims of other people's choices. God has given us the ability, however, to leave those things behind, to break away from such and to be free in our own right. The bad things that happen to us, they are not his fault because he gave us free will, he does not force us to walk in the path that he set for us humans to walk in. Sometimes, we disobey him and we walk in our own paths, then we prick our feet or even lose them, or we lose our lives. But, as long as we go back to the right path, it will take us to the right destination. You see, that path is always there. His love is always there for us ...'

She has already shut him out by the time that he finishes spewing out the very familiar dogma, but for the sake of respect she doesn't interrupt him. She is angry though, on the inside, towards herself for feeling this way, and towards this God of Reverend Mbudzi and Previous who has wonderful words and no action.

'Do you understand, my daughter?' he asks after his long explanation that fell on deaf ears.

She nods her head. She really can't wait for him to leave her alone.

He doesn't leave. He smiles.

'Your mother and Tribulation are here,' says Chipo, who all this time was sitting next to Reverend Mbudzi, saying nothing.

'I don't want to see them.'

'Please, my daughter, I beg you. If not for your sake, but for theirs, please let them see you,' Reverend Mbudzi pleads.

She agrees, grudgingly and to avoid another sermon.

Chipo runs out through the double doors and comes back with Mother and Tribulation. Reverend Mbudzi prays for Mercy, his eyes and those of the others closed, but hers wide open, before he walks away with Chipo and leaves Mother and Tribulation crying as they sit on the bench on the other side of the bars.

'Mother,' Tribulation keeps saying from his wheelchair. He says that and nothing more. Seeing him like this breaks Mercy's heart. She reaches out her fingers through the bars and he holds on to them until the guard says, 'Time is up.'

'One minute, please?' begs Mercy.

'Okay. One minute.'

Mother cries and fails to say anything to her daughter other than 'I am sorry.' Mercy gets it, she can see that she indeed is sorry, but what does sorry achieve? VaMusungwa used to say, 'sorry can't buy you a thing.'

'Me too, *mama*. I am sorry.'

Twenty-two

Lord of mercy

Big Maria has bullied Previous enough, Mercy decides. Who does she think she is? She watches her as she forces Previous to pick up sanitary pads from the floor with her bare fingers, as she forces her to wash her panties and as she urinates on her bible. Mercy has to stop this once and for all.

'Don't touch her again,' she demands.

'Or else?' Big Maria asks, breathing into Mercy's face.

'Or else I will kill you.'

'Well, good luck, b***h! Let's see who between you and me has the balls to do it. I, Big M, will have your head on a silver platter in no time at all, and we will have you for dinner.'

Mercy walks away, indignant but terrified, and Big Maria interprets it correctly; she is afraid and so can be bullied. So much for the one who killed a man and a woman and ate their flesh.

It is a Tuesday when this happens and that night, for no reason at all, Mercy decides that she will go to the church meeting in the small hall with Previous.

'Well done, Mercy,' says Previous. 'You won't regret it.'

'Don't be too happy, or else I won't go.'

She does go, however, and the church service is not bad after all. Most of the hymns and choruses which they sing are not new to her, she grew up hearing these, and Mother always had a tune on her lips when she was at home. It takes her right back to her childhood with Chipo and Freedom and Lovemore, to those days of innocence and mild mischief. She forgets for a moment the road that she has travelled and the transformation that she has gone through over the not-so-many years. The prison chaplain, Pastor Ndoro, and the visiting church, a Pentecostal one from Marondera, exude a great amount of joy like they are caught up in the seventh heaven. They sing and jump and dish out hope for free. The young men and women who share the message inspire her, they almost break through into the softer tissue of her hardened heart, but are only prevented by the manner of their ministry which reminds her of Munamato. She loves them, except for this. Her feelings are a glorious mixture of good and bad, like she is chewing tasty mushrooms seasoned with sand.

When they are on their way back to the cell, Mercy is uplifted in her spirit. 'Thank you, Previous,' she says.

'For what?'

'For inviting me.'

'Did I?'

'Not today of course, but you inspired me all the same.'

'You are welcome.'

They walk back to the cell, unaware of what is awaiting them. Mercy is the first one to find her blanket in a pool of water and to smell the faeces that have been buried inside it. Previous's is the same, and her underwear which she left hung out to dry has been dipped in urine. Surprisingly and unlike the other days, both Big Maria and Pams are fast asleep and snoring, as is as everyone else. Mercy is not fooled. She knows whose work this is. She is seized with an anger which out the glorious feeling from her heart. She pulls the blankets off of them and demands that they wake up. They don't move. Previous tries to restrain her from provoking them, but it is too late. Mercy is feeling very much like the lady who killed a man and a woman, the one she has pretended to be over the past few months. She has had enough.

'Wake up, Maria. Wake up!' she says as she pokes her with her foot.

Big Maria ignores her.

Mercy gathers the blankets in her arms and plunges them into Big Maria's face, pressing them against her nose and mouth. Big Maria is infuriated. She growls and howls like a dog and wakes up the rest of the girls she bullied into pretending that they were fast asleep. Rising up to her feet, she shoves Mercy with her right elbow as she spits all over the place. Mercy staggers and tumbles over the feet of those still lying on the floor. Regaining her balance and springing up to her feet, she rams into Big Maria like a female black rhino defending her calves, hitting Big Maria's head against the concrete walls in the back of the cell, causing her to thud against the floor. She sits on top of her and thumbs her face with her fists so fast that Big Maria has no chance at all to respond. Blood flows from her nose and messes up the floor as the other in-mates shout at the top of their voices in excitement, inviting the attention of the prison guards who come running and sound the siren.

The cell door still unlocked, the guards storm into the cell and pounce on Mercy, whose hands are now smeared with Big Maria's blood. They drag them both away into an office where they interrogate them. The decision goes against Mercy and she is taken into solitary confinement in the D section of the prison. There, in the little room not big enough even for one person, it is dark 24/7, the only light streaming through a hole far above, in the very high roof, during the day, and there are no blankets at all, not even the skinny and lice-infested red ones she is used to. She huddles herself into the corner for 48 hours with no sound or sense of time, only piecing this together from the meals which are delivered to her and pushed through the hole at the bottom of the heavy metal door which has been painted black. The only positive thing for her is that she has time to think about her life whilst she is in there, to reflect and to cry. She asks many questions to the walls around her, and to the God of Mother and Previous and Reverend Mbudzi.

'If you are there, then talk to me,' she says. 'Why do I have to suffer like this? What have I done that misfortune follows me?' She cries until her eyes are washed clean and she has released every emotion, yet still there is no answer for her.

On the second day, in the morning, she hears someone whispering out her name. For a moment she thinks her ears are deceiving her. She thinks that she is hallucinating as it surely can't be God answering her prayer. 'Who is it?' she asks.

'It's me. Previous.'

She is relieved. 'What are you doing here?' she asks.

'Cleaning the corridor.'

'Where is everybody?'

'In the fields. I will be out day after tomorrow, Mercy. God has heard my prayers.'

'How is that possible, Previous? You still have three years to go.'

'It's a miracle, Mercy. The news came yesterday. I have been given presidential pardon.'

'Good for you. I am happy for you.'

'Stay strong, Mercy, and remember there is a God who answers prayers.'

After Previous is gone, Mercy ponders about what she said to her. It is too good to be true, to imagine that one could be released from this hell of a place just like that. But then, Previous was really never in captivity although she was in prison like her. She seemed to be free all the time. Mercy figures that it is her that is truly in prison, that has been in prison since Father raped her, and is still there. She can't figure out how to be free, how to move on with life. Previous gives her hope. She pictures again in her mind, Reverend Mbudzi sitting on the other side of the bars and Mother and Tribulation crying, Tribulation saying 'mother' to her. There is a melting inside her heart and she begins to cry, silently. The tears that flow are pure and warm. She decides that she needs in her heart whatever Previous has in hers. She needs it if she is to survive this ordeal.

After a long time, she hears the chains of the huge door cling and the locks open. She stays put in the corner as the stout female guard, the one who looks like she eats all the food meant for the others, and a male one, stand at the door, a sudden light blinding her eyes.

'Come with us,' they demand.

They don't need to say it again. She struggles to her feet and follows them, rubbing her eyes. It is in the afternoon, unlike what she thought. The darkness inside the cell deceived her.

They transfer her to a different cell which has five other inmates, she being the sixth. They receive her warmly, partly because they are afraid of her, and mainly because they are not as bad a bunch as those in Big Maria's cell. Mercy recalls seeing three of them in the church a few days ago. They are singing a hymn. She joins in, at first just because she recognises the words, but later because she feels her heart sing along with them.

In the night, she sleeps like a baby.

On the morrow, when Previous is leaving, all clean, in her own clothes and free from the dirty uniform, she stops by Mercy's cell. They hold hands through the bars and cry.

'Bye, Mercy, and thanks for protecting me,' says Previous before she begins to walk away, the guard by her side.

Mercy feels her heart go after her. She can't let her go. 'Previous,' she calls after her.

Previous stops in the corridor and looks back at her, and so does the stout female guard.

'I want it. What you have, I want it too.'

Previous looks at the guard with begging eyes. The guard motions to her to do whatever she has to do, so she runs back to Mercy's new cell. Mercy kneels down on the inside, behind the bars, warm tears flowing down her face. Her cellmates sing a hymn for her; *Ndinoshamiswa kwazvo*, as Previous holds her hands through the bars and prays for her.

A warmth fill her heart, a lightness she has never felt before. When Previous is done praying, she knows that she too will make it. 'Thank you,' she says as she manages a smile. She senses that the load has been lifted from her, that a load of mercy has been poured upon her head. After all, Tinashe was right.

THE END

gcmazarura@gmail.com